Also by Tom Rapko

*Diving the Seamount*

# CORCOVADO

Tom Rapko

iUniverse, Inc.
New York   Bloomington

iUniverse books may be ordered through booksellers or by contacting:

iUniverse
1663 Liberty Drive
Bloomington, IN 47403
www.iuniverse.com
1-800-Authors (1-800-288-4677)

Because of the dynamic nature of the Internet, any Web addresses or
links contained in this book may have changed since publication and
may no longer be valid. The views expressed in this work are solely those
of the author and do not necessarily reflect the views of the publisher,
and the publisher hereby disclaims any responsibility for them.

ISBN: 978-1-4401-2206-4 (pbk)
ISBN: 978-1-4401-2207-1 (ebk)

Printed in the United States of America

iUniverse rev. date: 2/23/2009

To My Wife

<u>flu·vi·al gold</u> *n.* Granular gold deposited in riverbed sediment

# PART ONE

▼

## LIFE'S STRUGGLE

♠ ♥ ♣ ♦

DROOPY FERNS PARTED. Their long, thick stems pressed together as he pulled a makeshift sled through the jungle. The undergrowth was clogged with mud from the incessant rain and made the task nearly impossible. Above the sound of his tired, strained breathing came the distinct noise of suctioning feet moving through the muck. He sunk in knee deep and struggled to continue. Swarms of mosquitoes attached themselves to his exposed skin. The caked mud layered across his arms provided no relief. Undeterred, Declan trudged on through the jungle, step after suctioning step.

"Twenty more minutes," he thought, "and I'll make it into the clearing."

High above his muscled shoulders, freckled with droplets of sweat, the canopy screeched and screamed. The howler monkeys' rough moans echoed through the vegetation and rumbled amongst the tree trunks. Shrill, incessant twerps from pastel-colored birds pierced the subtle breeze. He stood weary in the heart of the Costa Rican jungle, utterly aware of his insignificance.

A pungent waft overwhelmed him, and before he saw them he smelled them; peccaries. Their signature odor of rotting fecal matter was unmistakable. It burned with an acidic swirl and wound its way down his throat. Disgusting. In the distance he heard snapping branches, snorting, and squealing. Declan wondered how many were in the herd. He eased his pace and moved forward cautiously, reaching the fringe of the clearing observant of any large, freestanding trees. Crouching to the ground, Declan peered through the underbrush. Runty legs, and hundreds of them, stomped in the clearing before him. Declan shook his head in a sarcastic grimace, watching in admiration as their primordial jaws clamped down on whatever happened to be on the ground, crushed it, and became part of their digestive track. The ultimate omnivores, these hairy jungle pigs ate fruit strewn on the ground, dug up roots, and tore the flesh off decomposing animals. At their most opportune moments, the peccaries would take down prey as large as a tapir. Several wallowed in stagnant pools of water at the buttress roots of ficus trees scratching their short swine fur. The trees provided a high canopy shielding the sun and simultaneously restricting the flow of fresh air.

Declan remained motionless, patiently waiting for them to leave. He hoped no fleeting breeze would betray his position. Ever-so-slowly, he backpedaled into the jungle. His skin crawled; he struggled to maintain his composure as he retraced his steps back into the jungle's protective fringe. He sat on his haunches until his knees hurt and then he shifted his weight to his ankles. His arms burned with an insatiable itch he dared not scratch. The peccaries razed the jungle floor, clearing and cleaning the green carpet like giant vacuums. Drops of sweat like foraging ants moved along his scalp. Declan didn't twitch.

After an agonizingly long time, the peccaries disbursed. One by one they disappeared back into the jungle foliage along narrow trodden paths formed by a thousand hooves over hundreds of years. The sloshing noises of their communal bathing stopped along with the sound of their shaking fur. Only their putrid stink of rotting flesh was left hovering in the air.

Easing from his position, Declan pulled his sled out of the rut and into the clearing. The stench convulsed his stomach. He dry heaved silently, covering his mouth with a salty forearm beaded with sweat, and pulled forward. The underwater dredge he towed remained secure with rubber ties used on 4 X 4 trucks. He had lassoed the dredge to a thick plastic sled designed for portage across the jungle floor. Its V-shaped kneel stretched along the base and cupped perfectly into the shallow molded plastic sled bottom. The design provided ideal support for the dredge and surprisingly good mobility in the jungle. It was hard work though, dragging this load through the thickness of the jungle. In his wake Declan left a serpentine path winding across the jungle floor.

The gasoline-powered prospecting dredge that sucked up all the sediment was anchored in the center of the sled. It was custom designed out of cast aluminum block for both weight and anti-corrosion considerations. Declan had outfitted the rear of the sled with four five-gallon plastic red containers. On the front of the sled he had lashed assorted diving equipment; two masks, a neoprene wet suit, worn gloves, booties, and a hookah regulator set-up along with a host of spare parts. A bright yellow plastic case protected his mobile laboratory which could perform small batch assay work as well as his laptop, additional batteries, and GPS equipment. On his back Declan carried a field hammock, food, and limited clothing supply. He'd been "in-country" for two weeks now and was meandering out of the jungle to run additional tests on the soil samples duct-taped to his hairy chest.

A furtive snap opened his lighter. Its bright blue flame came to life instantly. The lighter worked in the most inhospitable conditions and needed next to nil in maintenance. After passing through the last pool he felt them crawling up his leg. Gelatinous blobs of sucking flesh wobbled on his skin. He pulled up his trousers past the sock line. Holding the lighter level, leech after leech seared off his body. They fell to the ground like shriveled raisins. A tube of insect cream a week empty came into his hands and he squeezed out the very last remnants over his fresh scabbed skin. His limbs burned. Declan winced at the number of whelps on his arms and legs; nearly all of the skin was checkered with bites and the mud splatter just seemed to irritate the skin more. A soft squeal echoed in his mind.

Declan turned his head instinctively toward the noise. Three feet away from him, a young peccary emerged from a watering pool. Its white lips trembled in fear. Declan put his index finger to his mouth motioning the pig to keep quiet. The piglet raised its brown and white snout. Twitching back and forth rapidly, it sampled the air. Suddenly, the baby peccary let fly a piercing scream. Declan hastily slung on his backpack and reached for the handles of the sled, but it was too late now and he knew it.

The peccary unwound another agonizing squeal. Declan knew how far and fast the shrill whine would carry. He palmed the hilt of the machete sheathed at his hip. Frozen in terror without its mother, the little pig was trembling. It squealed again and the clearing erupted with screaming banshees. From every conceivable direction white-lipped peccaries came running into the clearing. Declan scanned the horizon and spotted his target. He dashed instinctively for the nearest load-bearing tree. They were on him at once. Adrenaline fired into his muscles, pumping his body chock-full of instant energy. He sped forward. In his first seven steps a dozen peccaries closed half the distance to him. Declan leapt over a bramble of thick ferns, stumbled, and reached for a tree limb. It was slippery and engulfed with prickly vines. No matter, he heaved forward.

His fingers clawed for traction with fingernails digging deep into the bark. Declan's upper body flared to life. His muscled torso was already halfway up the limb. He anchored his first foot as a wedge into the base trunk and pushed up. He was fast, but not fast enough. Just as one foot swung up securely, an intense pain shot through his other calf. He stumbled and slipped. Blinding light flashed into Declan's eyes. His forehead jabbed into another of the tree's limbs. He grappled higher into the tree, lunging for a better stand.

Clutching a branch, Declan pulled himself up. A peccary dangled on him. He reached for the machete slug along his waist. In one swift motion he unsheathed and swung the stone-sharpened blade at his leg. Declan smashed the peccary squarely between the eyes with a distinctive "thwack!" The mangled jaws stopped sputtering saliva. Declan pried the pig's cracked skull off his leg using the machete as a crowbar and let the carcass drop to the jungle floor. A ruckus of fifty peccaries circled below, quickly devouring their bloody comrade. Only clumps of fur and bone too thick to chew remained. They peered up at Declan with enraged swine eyes. Trampling along a tree limb that served as a bridge, another brute came at him. Declan wedged his back against the trunk and pushed. The fallen limb creaked, and then fell with a leafy, bustling rush toward the jungle floor. The peccary sped forward and leapt. Declan whirled the machete across his chest, cut through the beast's ribcage, and impaled the peccary against the trunk through his heart. The peccary persisted, even as it expired, to gnaw at Declan.

A curtain of blood obscured Declan's sight. His muddy fingers brushed aside the sticky goo, streaking it across his brow. He felt his forehead. A deep gash from his hairline stretched down to his eyebrow. It bled profusely. The pain, though, actually pulsed from his leg. He looked down and saw a gaping wound on the inside of his calf. The throbbing sensation was intense. The skin was jagged, torn in triangular shards and peeled back like a potato skin. Bright aerated blood oozed down his leg. Drip by drip, his blood formed a crimson pool in the middle of the tree's emerald moss. Declan heard the characteristic grinding of bone below. The peccaries finished off their fellow herdsman.

He slumped his head back against the trunk and felt his feet fall out from under him. As he faded in and out of consciousness, he thought he heard the sound of plastic scrapping. But how could that be? Declan didn't have any plastic on him, the only plastic items he could think of were the portable assay equipment boxes on his sled.

♠ ♥ ♣ ♦

FIERY EYES DILATED as the full sun descended into dusk. Four fingers fashioned with suction knobs on their tips provided inseparable traction on the leaf's stem. He rested his soft underbelly on the stem and listened intently to all that was going on around him waiting patiently for the tell-tale buzz, vibration, or scent which would signal dinner. Thin, rubbery legs with flashy red feet hung down from a muscled bodice. He raised one purple thigh, twice again his body length, up to the stem's perch and waited. His other limb dangled from the stem and swayed in the breeze.

Birds soaring in the pastel skies circled their final laps and came in to roost. Minutes later the first chatter of nesting birds began easing day into night. A milky dusk settled on the horizon, dipping the greenery in a golden halo. The dangers of the jungle lurked everywhere, yet a silent respite seemed to fill the air. The jungle cats purred awake, bats rustled, and a thousand other creatures calling this habitat home prepared for the transition.

He leapt into the air seemingly defying gravity. Gliding high, he extended a thin tongue far into the distance. Its barbed edges tore into the moth's velvety blue wings, wrapped around its body and whipped back almost instantly into the red-eyed tree frog's mouth. Sleek pads stretched forward and he grabbed the shallow branch. The frog landed gently, bounced softly, and deftly climbed to a better observation post. Within minutes he sat perched high in the canopy surveying Corcovado as the last rays of sunlight fell from the sky and revealed the early evening stars again.

Off in the distance, on the water's edge, a thin fog silently brewed as the land cooled faster than the sea. A high, lone cloud danced above the rippling waves. It drifted down, misted the jungle with the nutrients of the sea, and scampered off. Leatherback hatchlings waddled along the beach and into the sea. And in that intersection of sea, sand, and jungle frenzied insect hunting began. The caves emptied. Furry wings slapped in the air, bats flooded the sky, and the night was suddenly filled with a hundred thousand sonar beams.

The presence of pura vita encapsulated him; the air, sea, and very land formed discernible boundaries of pure form and function. For a time the red-eyed tree frog remained motionless, waiting again for the perfect moment to strike. His thick black pupils pushed aside the red in his eyes as he scanned the canopy for airborne meals. And they came with a rhythmic certainty.

As night unfurled her blanket of afternoon clouds, she cooled the muggy air. The red-eyed tree frog kept his vigil, occasionally shifting his position by grappling up along the limb or shimmying down an errant vine when a meal approached. His frog tummy grew plump. Insidiously, he succumbed to a comatose trance induced by blood rushing to digest the nocturnal feast. But he was not the only hunter.

Horned eyebrows lifted ever-so-slowly. Slithering forward with a depressed pit between its eyes, the snake detected the slightest temperature variance a mere yard away. Tactile golden scales held the coiled viper's tail taunt on the limb, while its upper shank loosened. A seamless muscular body sprang. Instinctively, the palm viper extended to full body length. As majestic as a golden bolt of lightning, its levered head flashed fangs toward the red-eyed tree frog. A millisecond passed before the viper reached full stretching distance. The red-eyed tree frog leapt desperately into the oblivion. No terrestrial support lay below him. The viper's jaws came crashing down, empty!

The red-eyed tree frog reached blindly for something to break his fall. There was nothing in his flight path. He hurdled toward the earth. He grasped for anything to snag, contorting his body to smash against a tree trunk in the black void around him. He fell and fell until hooking an errant baby vine saved him. It slowed him just enough before it broke to alter his fall onto a soft, muddied cotton shirt soaked with blood. The next thing the tree frog remembered was being lifted onto a refreshing, wet leaf by two gigantic animal paws oddly devoid of fur.

Declan stood from his kneeling position. Light was slowly coming across the sky. It was still dark, but the birds were awake chirping in chorus. He watched as the gorgeous red-eyed tree frog looked back at him as he hopped away. Declan found the fellow cemented to his chest.

Declan eased his way down the tree. He slung his backpack over a tree limb and tied it there. He reached in a side pouch and took out his water bottle.

The faithful plastic bottle remained as secure and unbreakable as ever. He unscrewed the opaque bottle's blue cap and let the water flow down his throat. Even iodine-laced water tasted good now.

He looked down at his calf and shook his head knowing full well it was already infected and a weeklong regiment with antibiotics was about to ensue, assuming he could get back of course. Pressure on his leg revealed its stiffness, but nothing was broken. Some of the muscle, though, was missing.

Declan scanned the ground looking for his gear. It wasn't too hard to find in the clearing.

The scattered gear that previously resided in the yellow hard case apparently had been of some interest to the peccaries, they managed not only to open the case, but gnaw every instrument into plastic pieces the size of Legos. His laptop, GPS, and portable assay kit were all destroyed and along with them, his hand-drawn maps littered the canopy floor like shreds of toilet paper. All in all it was a depressing sight.

The dredge was largely intact but the scuba gear remained incognito. Declan flipped his wrist and checked the time. The sun mirrored the plastic and he saw his head gash in the reflection for the first time. He forgot about the head wound; he likely wouldn't do that again because its depth and length would remind him, and his buddies, for some time of this incident. He smiled to himself. Piece by piece, he picked up the rubbish which had been his equipment and loaded it on the sled. After fifteen minutes of cleaning up Declan redoubled his efforts and pushed out. He moved once again toward the water.

It took another half an hour to clear the brush, but he finally made it to the shore, at which point he remembered his backpack. It was still tied to the tree branch! He shook his head, limped back into the jungle and found his bag just where he had left it earlier. By ten o'clock he finally organized all of his gear on the beach and took a break to eat. All that remained was a handful of protein bars and iodine water. He ate the bars and drank the iodine water from the bottle. Declan pulled out his binoculars, stood on the sled over the dredge, and surveyed the coast.

The water was liquid jade, opaque near the shore and a translucent blue beyond the churning barrier reef. It contrasted markedly with the jungle's layered leafy green. Errant waterways lapped on and off the beach, forming discernable inlets varying from the width of a footbridge to the girth of entire soccer field. Rolling shambles of well-worn rocks, tumbled as smooth as talc, layered many of the deepest inlets transitioning land to sea. The surf was loud. Surging waves crested, and then smashed again the barrier reef. As the waves eased back to the open sea, wisps of sea foam floated in the air and came to rest like champagne bubbles on the sand. The sea foam sparkled and glimmered in the daylight like the shores of El Dorado. It was here, squinting, Declan spied the inlet where he had left his kayak stowed.

With little ado, he anchored the dive dredge high on the beach wedging it against the jungle's fringe using the remains of his rubber ties to securely root-fasten it. He remembered his pack this time and hobbled along to the inlet.

The distance to the inlet where his kayak lay perched was deceptive. There was no easy way to make a vertical point-to-point walk, the jagged coast required constant switchbacks and numerous wades into the salt water. Though disinfecting on his open wound, it wasn't quite refreshing. In what seemed like hours, finally he reached the inlet and thankfully his kayak remained secure high in a tree awaiting his return. Limping as he worked, Declan made a mental note to enjoy as much wild boar as his stomach could handle when he returned to San Jose. Inevitably, he knew an antibiotic drip lay in his future. Having suffered a similar, if less dramatic, mishap on a coral reef in Australia had taught him anything it was this; get his leg treated as soon as possible.

Declan monkeyed up the tree, slashed the binders, and eased his kayak down. He saddled up his gear quickly, let the kayak drift into knee-deep water, and finally pushed off.

♠ ♥ ♣ ♦

It was slow going trying to break away from the surf. Even at full physical capacity he knew this trek would have still taken the better part of six hours. Given his current condition he doubted he'd pull in before sundown, assuming he could last that long. Declan believed ocean kayaking was tedious business best left to endurance rowers.

A continuous, suffering cycle of paddling ultimately broke Declan away from the surf. He kept pace in the open ocean at a steady and sustainable rate. Beyond the shore's surge, the water lapsed calmly. Declan soon found himself paddling at a nice clip. "Splash, splash," it sounded when he mistimed the row, otherwise it was a silent "dip, dip" into the ocean that pushed his craft along the rich coast. Along his flanks dive birds stole fish from the Pacific. Parallel to the shore, he trudged on and on. The incessant paddle became his rhythm, a trance he fell into and barely lifted his head from the horizon.

Below the kayak, schooling baitfish kept time with his paddles. They clustered in a tight ball and took comfort in the shade the kayak provided from the day's noon sun. The blazing yellow star was perched high in the sky and only a handful of white cumulus clouds hovered in the air. The sun's rays smothered the coast with an equatorial heat. It was a warmth that made Declan feel woozy.

Three hours into the paddle he pulled ashore for a lunchtime "power nap." It lasted until dusk. His leg was getting progressively worse, and he estimated at this point he was only a quarter of the way back to Drake Bay. Declan gathered up his gear and pitched what would suffice for his evening lodging against the backdrop of the jungle. It was a sandy beachhead adequately above the waterline, protected from the elements, and a decent overnight camp. His metallurgical expedition was starting to look a lot less profitable as the possibility of mortality played its hand.

Declan foraged nearby for clumps of driftwood that had washed up along the coastline, separating the useful dry slivers from damp logs. All along the beach clumps of wood long since separated from their source lined the entrance to the jungle. They were perched evenly on the high-water mark of the incoming tide for the year, serving as a definitive barometer noting where the water had gone highest and had since lapsed. There were entire trees, rooted and all, along with scatterings of branches, leafed-palms, and the occasional milled plank.

Before the sun fell, he had assembled a respectable pile of starter and night wood. Declan grimaced as he bent over to start the fire. A waterproof match, constant companion ever since the time he was caught overnight in Monteverde with a broken ankle, came to life. It was no substitute for the lighter he lost, but it got the job done, and well. The starter shards sparkled then took. The fire came alive. Declan fed the night wood into the fire. It threw off the warmth his shaking body craved. Even in the jungle, he knew, the coolness at night could be unbearable, especially along the water. Declan fell in and out of consciousness as he drifted off to sleep after finishing the last of his food reserves and pounded an iodine-laced nightcap.

His dreams were those of a feverish man; illogical and highly realistic. Profuse amounts of sweat launched him well on the way to dehydration before midnight. His past came back to him and he went back to his past; to mistakes he'd made and remedies implied. He rolled a thousand grains of sand with each toss and turn of the jungle mat he'd made for himself. And in the early depths of night, he started shaking uncontrollably.

Cold shivers are one thing, but this was another. His body convulsions shook him awake and he found himself drenched in sweat. With blurred vision, he was barely able to stand.

Declan decided he would have to make a leap of faith and press onward immediately. Without a second thought, he abandoned his gear and bumbled down off the beachhead toward his kayak.

With only the light of the moon, he pushed off. He paddled in and out of the beach surf until he was sure he was clear of it all. The water was rough, so it took him twice as long as the day before to clear it.

Fierce white surf crashed on either side of him as he cleared past its treachery and into the open blue depths. He kept the faithful coastline, black against the light of the moon, to the right of his shoulder as his unassailable mental compass. Declan paddled for a time, then slumped over in exhaustion.

The water below him was alive. Perhaps sea turtles were swimming back out to sea, maybe a pod of dolphins were testing his nerve, or as his mind rightly imagined, a bull shark had scented upon his bloody chum line. He paddled on, soldiering from one hour to the next until the sun rose and blanketed his body with a motherly warmth.

According to his watch he had been paddling since two, now it was just past six. With the three hours yesterday he reckoned he must surely be upon Drake Bay. The delightful light illuminated the contours of the coastline, and indeed, he had entered the sheltered bay some time ago.

He was now on a beeline to civilization, and as he would later recall, the means to get help. Along the final stretch his thirst was unbearable, twice he briefly lost consciousness. Finally, Declan docked in Drake Bay. The doctor was immediately summoned. In the interim, Declan was served ginger tea. It was hot, acidic, and burned his throat with each swallow. Somehow this was supposed to help cool his fever. He was too weary to protest.

He drifted in and out of consciousness as a full fever took hold of him. A missionary nurse claimed he died, but her finger on his pulse had simply proven too weak. The local doctor gave him oral antibiotics, which Declan threw up, and put him on the next flight into San Jose.

The single engine prop sped down the improvised runway, burn-cut from the depths of the jungle just surpassing two thousand feet, and the young pilots choked the choke up tight. The blades whined miserably and the plane took to the air. Fixed landing gear cleared the rocky shore without a nick this time. They circled once and then ascended into a cloudy day. Misty air obscured the mountains around them.

Tips flashed green suddenly, then faded just as quickly. The vegetation was literally a soup of greens and poking ferns, textures and elevations that jutted out of the landscape. A flight path flown a thousand times descended into the regional airport after less than thirty minutes. Declan wasn't the only pale-faced passenger on this flight; a flight he vaguely remembers getting on, but never getting off.

♠ ♥ ♣ ♦

"WHERE AM I?" Declan opened his mouth before his eyes.

Bright white lights blinded him. "Nietzsche was right," he mumbled, "the abyss does stare back at you!"

He squinted to keep the receptors in his eyes from completely burning out. He instinctively reached for his chest. The duct-taped pouch was gone! He felt around his bed for a call button. "Nurse? Nurse?" he grumbled.

"Un Momento!" an answer blared back to him as he overheard rushed footsteps in the background. A congregation of white-soled feet entered his room all at once.

"Oh, you have become conscious!" exclaimed a beaming young nurse in broken English.

"Apparently," Declan started and looked at all the surprised attendants, "and do any of you know the location of a small leather pouch that I had taped to my chest?" He suspected someone knew, because a significant amount of chest hair had been removed along with the duct tape and pouch.

Just then, a shapely doctor came in the room followed by a green-suited man identified by his uniform as a ranger of the National Parks Service.

"It wouldn't be this leather pouch would it?" The park ranger let a soft beige draw-string pouch dangle from his hand.

"Salvador please," the female doctor interrupted, "Mr. Mares you have been with fever for two straight days and as you can tell you're now receiving intravenous antibiotics. I'm sorry about your leg, we did the best we could...given the circumstances."

Suddenly the collegial jokes about the peccaries Declan had imagined didn't seem so funny. Below his knee he felt a throbbing sensation. It burned bad, real bad.

Declan clutched the bedspread with his free arm and flung the sheet off his body with one motion. It swept full like the sail of a ship and gently glided down to the floor.

And there, below his knee where once a muscled leg stood, was a reconstructed calf. Half of it was gone entirely, and the rest he imagined under the bandages jimmied together. He was right, several hundred zigzagging blue stitches had been used.

"Hey," Salvador Maria Antonio got his attention, "I know what you're doing...you...," he hesitated for just an instant, "jungle diver, but keep that out of my park!" Salvador Maria Antonio shook his head and motioned to leave the room, but stopped at the door. Salvador Maria Antonio's weathered hands removed the pouch from his pocket, "take your souvenir and go home. Those rivers have many secrets...at least live to tell yours."

Salvador Maria Antonio looked at Declan, grinned with a sparkling gold tooth, and placed the pouch on an attending table. With a push he wheeled it over to Declan and walked out of the room.

# PART TWO

▼

## LIFE'S PASSION

♠ ♥ ♣ ♦

Pastel mascara painted their delicate wings. And just after the heavy rains, when the air was still thick with the temptation of floral nectar, they took to the sky. The butterflies rode on the warm westerly breeze high into the canopy above. Here they fluttered along the treetops and PhD candidate Lauren McAlister sat perched overlooking the vast greenery carpeting the earth as far as the eye could see just for this purpose.

She had inched her way up the trunks of over a dozen trees. During her many days in the jungle she had strung a canopy line traversing them all in a thin, metallic human spider web that interlocked all the surrounding trees into one large aerial observatory. From her vantage Lauren swooped down through the height of the clouds and observed her precious lepidoptera.

Feigning a thousand things they were not, from owls' eyes to snake heads, the butterflies proved to be master illusionists. Lauren's gloved hands gripped the brake as she descended rapidly from the canopy. The jungle floor rushed up towards her. Over the zipping sound of the rope she heard the scarlet macaws screeching in a loose formation above her. They weaved into the shadows of a fruit tree and landed there temporarily.

Lauren's forearms were freckled with stains from the dripping berries the jungle denizens consumed above her, as was her wide straw hat that screened her fair skin from the equatorial sun. As she drew closer to the jungle floor, sweeping lush ferns and leaves as large as umbrellas greeted her descent.

Gently she eased to earth and unclamped the descender. She loosened the straps along her thighs where the harness had secured her waist to the safety lines. Her frame was lean and muscular, but interestingly enough, feminine all at the same time; a distinction never lost on the opposite sex. The jungle's humidity unwound her coiled cinnamon curls into natural auburn waves. Lauren's irises mirrored the jungle's light green foliage and bloomed whenever they left the jungle floor to ascend into the canopy. Barring a small blemish on her front tooth from a rock climbing fall, Lauren's smile was flawless. Her face was calming, intelligent, and had the contours of strength about it.

Lauren packed her gear into a large black tote-bag and grabbed her backpack. Slinging it over her shoulder, she decided to make her way back. The mid-day sun, remaining high and hot, reminded her of a Finnish sauna, complete with the snapping tree branch wands. It was near impossible not to walk through some distance of growth as the trail dipped in and out of existence every couple yards. She looked over her shoulder from whence she came and peered above where all her tree stands remained fastened.

She had constructed a city here in the depths of the jungle. For several hundred yards strategically placed lifts, ledges, swings, cables, and mountings were secured along a shallow ridge-line.

Lauren studied, collected, and most importantly thought about her work along this course of foliage. She was passionate about her career and it showed. Lauren remained longer, climbed higher, and challenged herself to find the truth. More than passion, it was an obsession, and one that she had tasted early in her college years and become totally enraptured with by the time she finished graduate school. And now it was simply her life, a life dedicated to understanding the intricacies of leopardry which, while mildly amusing to perhaps the novice or an urbanite slaving away in some office, was her totality. And like most things in which we find ourselves in love with, Lauren was very, very good at what she did.

As an authority in the field, her papers had grown steadily to fill some of the most prestigious scientific journals. In and out of her specialty, it was not uncommon for scientists to recognize her by name at social events. Lauren was slightly famous. Often when fortune smiles upon youth early it proves to be a dark omen, but in Lauren's case the little notoriety she gained in her zoological pursuits vaulted her career. Even so, she never was one to believe fully about what others said about her not matter how glowing. This made her antagonists practically helpless.

Lauren marched to her own beat, oftentimes in the face of convention. Probably this is why many men found her so difficult, or "challenging," to be with; she regarded her personal freedom highly and although compromise professionally was quite possible, in relationships with the men of academia in her life proved to be just the opposite. She cared little, though, as she found comfort in her work, she said so publicly, and was sustained by her personnel adventures.

Lauren proceeded down the trail, but made a sharp turn at the colloquially termed "bastard tree," due to its progressive spines porcupining off the tree's trunk. She came upon a stream and did a switchback along its length. The trail wound up higher and higher.

The air grew a touch thinner. Even the jungle trees for all their might could not consummate the canopy fully above her now as the width of the river increased and a noticeable divide formed on the two sides of the jungle. Lauren stopped to remove her hiking boots on the ledge above the river and put on a pair of her Teva sandals.

Lauren descended down the trail. She sloshed along the edge of the river enjoying the scenery and keeping an eye out for the lizards dashing across the top of the water. Their long, thin tails whipped back and forth giving the viewer the distinct impression that the lizard was in fact walking on water. Aptly named the "Jesus Christ lizard," it often did seem to have the ability to walk on water at great length, across a river for instance, and skip happily onwards when the opposite shoreline was reached. For her part, Lauren simply enjoyed the beauty found so abundant not only in the jungle, but particularly along the water.

The flowing noise of the river was replaced with a thundering crackle characteristic of tumbling stones. Before her stood a tremendous rocky outcropping. It rose over two hundred feet into the air. Laddered in pool after pool of rainwater, the sculpted ledge provided a magnificent dream of cascading ponds glistening in the sunlight.

She meandered her way along the river's edge. It became difficult now as the river had narrowed and the current increased. Lauren spotted her landmark ahead, a monolithic boulder jutting up seemingly from the center of the earth.

The black nylon tote with all her personal climbing equipment, day samples, and a host of smaller accoutrements rubbed alongside her waist. Lauren was officially hot now, and the ring of sweat along her armpits and back darkened her grey shirt. She unscrewed her water bottle and drank deeply.

Lauren lassoed her hair back into a tight pony tail. Without a cursory glance around, she rolled off her shirt, unhitched her bra, and peeled off her underwear. At once her body was naked, save for her Tevas, in the sweltering jungle heat.

The moisture beaded on her skin. The thought of the cool water seemed more pleasurable than ever. She walked along the delicate trail that arched above the pool careful not to slip along the earthen path fringed with emerald moss. Thick and rich, the jungle floor had seemingly laid a footpath along the pool's rim. She eased her body into the water.

She slipped into the water just past her navel and felt the cool sensation rise along her thighs. Her frequent jungle swims had taught her to always wear her Tevas for protection against a rocky bottom and an infrequent interlude when the occasional jungle guest wanted a sip of water. The sandals made for a quick exit if necessary. Lauren moved past the wadding area and fully submerged herself in the tranquil water.

She swam deeper using frog kicks to propel her to the bottom of the pool. The water was markedly cooler there and goose bumps dotted her skin. She touched bottom for an instant then surged to the surface with a triumphant splash.

Lauren succumbed to the beauty of the pool and bobbed carelessly on the surface. With her back parallel to the earth, she gazed up expectantly toward the sky. The waterfall high above her misted jungle water into the air. Wisps of moisture sparkled and danced their way down upon her. The falling water had originated higher still in the thickly vegetated hills where pools of rain came over the long track of rocky knolls and rich volcanic soil. From their fissures issued a quartet of discrete chirping noises so common of the beautiful jungle birds. Here their nests were safe, in the very areas large animals dared not venture and away from predators from the air who could not discern the fragile life being nurtured by the water of life.

The water gathered momentum, met with its compadres, and pushed ahead with more spirit still. Under the roots, but above the semblance of bedrock, it followed its own course until it could tolerate the subterranean world no longer. It came upon the hillside and culminated with a sustained burst high over the precipice.

Above her an ocean of blue intermingled with wisps of white and filled the horizon as far and wide as she could see. Eddies of water twirled around her skin. For some time she floated leisurely around the pool, but at length Lauren felt cold and thought better to start hiking back to camp. She paddled over to the lip of the pool and exited with a quick, noiseless splash.

Her form and function embraced pura vita. Droplets of rain, a cool breeze, and even the sun's rays always fell particularly well upon her skin. Uncanny as it sounds, she was at once always of and in nature; thus there should be no surprise in the advantage bestowed on her by the jungle. She roamed free, wild, without care save for her research and was by all means a woman who loved life, and by all accounts, it loved her. And that, amongst other things, made Lauren a very rare butterfly indeed.

She came full circle around the earthen crevasse. It was here she was allowed access to the swimming hole. Her clothing lay as she left it, spread on the volcanic rock speckled with hints of obsidian. Wherever her tan ended, her porcelain skin contrasted markedly with the blackness of the rock. The contrast was so severe it appeared almost as paper on charcoal. Lauren spread her towel on the rock, removed her Tevas and pulled on her clothing. It clung uncomfortably to her skin on the way up. She undid the tie on her hair and quickly restored the auburn locks to their rightful color with the help of her towel. With her pack loosely on her shoulder, Lauren headed to base camp satiated by the jungle.

♠ ♥ ♣ ♦

THE EXECUTIVE COMMITTEE sat comfortably on the top floor of International Petroleum Exploration & Extraction Co. (IPEEC) sifting through a dozen development proposals. The board had on its mind expansion plans into second and third world countries, politically termed "emerging markets," whose growth prospects seemed particularly viable. The race for energy resources had become extremely keen in light of a seemingly insatiable global demand.

Countries throughout the world, and particularly the mega-populous states, had seen an exponential increase in the resources they consumed. Driving all of this real estate, manufacturing, and service growth was oil. It paled in comparison to only perhaps the sun in driving the Earth's industrialized growth over the ages.

China and India had entered their own industrial revolutions, revolutions carried out with populations totaling over 2.6 billion people combined. And what these populations desired, no craved, was oil. Oil, the toxic, black poisonous lifeblood of humanity's growth. It would be refined, reformulated, altered, morphed, into thousands of products. Many of these products were wholly different from their source, allowing man to create seemingly better and better technologies. And this commodity had now fully begun to change the attitudes and behavior the masses struggling to lead a better life. As millions of poor sought refuge in the opportunity of a better life they sought material satisfaction. And this material satisfaction came at an expense. The expense was in the form of the bile black god.

This was the campaign story at least, the story the American people were continuously assuaged with, reality lay elsewhere. Reality that clearly, irrefutably, illustrated that 4% of the world's population consumed 25% of the petro. Of that quarter world consumption, only 30% was met by domestic production. This thirsty beast now prowled the world in search of its next victim, and devoured everything in its sight, slurping up pools of shallow finds here and drilling to the center of the earth for hitherto unreachable tracks.

One emerging market prospect seemed particularly tantalizing; a potentially large crude deposit in the only stable Central American country that also possessed both an educated, but cheap, workforce and a viable seaway to export this liquid treasure north for IPEEC's refineries in the Gulf of Mexico, Texas, or even California. On the polished steel and glass table a topographic map was spread open.

A projection screen above displayed a three dimensional core sampling report. One of IPEEC's teams from OilFinder™, a software program harnessing the power of supercomputing Cray computers, had returned recently with convincing test data obtained from a deep trek into the Costa Rican jungle reserve of Corcovado. Though by no means absolutely conclusive, the images displayed indicated enough to further discuss the possibility of sending a better equipped team back down with the resources to prove the find. If indeed the data suggested correctly, IPEEC stood on nearly twenty years of proven reserves. Twenty years of proven reserves for the world!

To help alleviate environmental concerns, the team would be dually tasked with gathering a chemical analysis of several flora and fauna substrates for a pharmaceutical company they were allied with in a seemingly an incestuous board-member swapping arrangement, dubbed interlocking, in which most Fortune 500 companies frequently engaged. This ruling elite collusively prevented competition to their respective industries by forming lucrative alliances with industry leaders diametric to their own. Assembling diversified teams and shipping them globally in search of conglomerate interests had proven to be a stroke of genius that was a necessary evil.

Under the auspices of their cloaked teams, the companies were able to divine valuable information on projects ranging from commodities demand (copper, nickel, steel) to even such things as the spread of viral agents. The collective corporations had each supplied six of their top field researchers along with an apprentice who had not yet reached that level of academia prominence, but served as a goodwill ambassador of sorts from a variety of undergraduate university programs to add further legitimacy to the expedition.

The conglomerates then brought these professors, scientists, and goodwill ambassadors together, formed them into appropriate teams, and financed their explorations under a variety of monikers, from archeological foundations to conservation non-profits to gain entrance to the some of the most remote, protected areas. Teaming proved to be the best way to remove personal accountability and any possible connection to the conglomerates' vested interests.

So an article that may have been published in a newspaper, for example, may very well have been written by a media company in partnership with an international oil company whose funds met the hands of a medical research company interested in the anthropology of an obsolete civilization needing advanced electronics of a defense contractor. Of course this was the story behind the story, what the reader, the consumer, read was a holistic endeavor to make their lives better through research of a university sponsored project.

Sarbanes-Oxley was supposed to have corporate governance transparent and held executive management both legally and personally responsible for stated financial performance. In some ways it increased accountability, yet this board of directors, like nearly every other one at major corporations, sat firmly entrenched in their positions since each sat on one another's board making the intricate web of old boy and wanton women network extremely difficult to unravel and harder still to "pin."

They acted on their own accord, supposedly under the purview of an impartial director's position, but reality dictated otherwise as even their director's very seats were in essence conflicts of interests. And there were many interests, with one interest rivaling that of all the others. Profit ruled king, prince to the paupers, and queen to the masses. The breadth and depth of their influence remains unfathomable; from energy, agriculture, and health care in which the medication you can take to the doctor who prescribes it are all part of the conglomerate's needlework.

Aptly termed "El Tigre," this expedition seemed like the perfect plan for the group; multiple opportunities in an environment they could operate freely with quick access to the findings and faster yet response to development if indeed they struck black gold. As an added twist, they came up with the idea of using a marine research vessel to park off the coast to help assuage fears by conservationists that their team would make an impact on the environment surrounding Cerro Tigre. All the testing and communications equipment would be on board the ambiguously named 120 ft. research vessel *Modern Explorer*. She was a beautiful vessel equipped to stand rough water and had made numerous expeditions throughout the world in search of one treasure or another. Board members of the International Petroleum Exploration and Extraction Co. remained silent as the team's leader, Dr. Vlacik, "Pickle" to his friends, bored into the briefing.

The old man knew his stuff. His experience working in the Central American region was virtually unrivaled. He had been in the early days working for several quasi-governmental organizations routing cargo from Colombia and Panama. When the action got too hot, he moved operations far enough south to keep out of the radar sweep that had brewed around the fringes of the cartels. As these short-lived empires collapsed under the pressure from the juggernaut to the north, Pickle sought employment from increasingly more reliable, if not legal, patrons who discretely overlooked his unwritten past.

Exposed skin on his face and hands dated Dr. Vlacik significantly older, however, than he really was, a mistake young crewmen never made twice. Quick and lean, his wiry body had been honed by repetitive, compulsive, exercise regimes molding him into peak conditioning. His intellect was no less impressive. His PhD and MD degrees, both from Yale, gave him instant credibility and a diversity of interests from which he was never without a comment or opinion.

"Ladies and Gentlemen," Pickle spoke softly and occasionally mumbled his presentations. His skill lay in accomplishing the various missions to which he was assigned, not in his personal delivery style which bordered on the verge of "mad scientist," though, he never lost his cool. Ever. And perhaps that was Dr. Vlacik's weakness, his compulsory methodology in which every aspect of his life was arranged and performed.

He continued with a short rasp, "as you can see in the above projections, our advance team has made quite the little data find. Their information suggests a moveable feast of dead dinosaurs lurking in the depths of years' past. Follow along my laser pointer and looking where the seismic pooling seems most reliable. It catches the eye, doesn't it? Bubbles of that magnitude necessitate on-site verification, verification that takes time to do correctly. That is why we must, absolutely must, be coy with our endeavor. *Modern Explorer* needs to be fully equipped for its cover, down to the association with named archeologists and respected members of the international regulatory bodies. We will need to rely on our members who are dually trained to be the eyes and ears on the ground. Instrument use, it goes without saying, is to be sanctioned only for the shadow teams. The more believable the further we get along, but all belief must end as there is nothing of value besides what lies underneath at Cerro Tigre."

Dr. Vlacik pulled into his suit breast pocket and palmed a thin leather case. He flipped open the hood and removed a thick, hand-rolled cigar. He cut it and puffed nonchalantly into the air. Boney hands from the board rose. Pickle dismissed their questions one at a time until after nearly an hour the Q & A session came to an abrupt halt and silence permeated the conference room. The ash tray was swollen full with a cone of ash.

"Very well, Dr. Vlacik. Take *Modern Explorer* south into Costa Rican waters. Our PR department will have drafted and released your cover. Six weeks, that's all we can spare to either confirm or disprove this claim," the talking head sat squarely in the middle of the directors.

"Six weeks is not enough!" Dr. Vlacik stood up from his position and waved his hands in protest.

"Six weeks is what you get," shot back the director.

Vlacik stood fully from his hunched position, grabbed his notes, and left the room without a word. Ten steps outside the meeting his cell phone was already on and he began barking instructions to his trusted lieutenants. They had better get their gear on order and a list of researchers, bona fide to be sure, ready on his beck and call as they would be pushing out earlier than expected if he was going to have more than six weeks to study Cerro Tigre. Dr. Vlacik's sharp teeth gleamed.

♠ ♥ ♣ ♦

THEY STOLE THROUGH Corcovado. A tense feeling of the chase was upon them. Brambling vines, errant boulders, and the thick, wet vegetation made their flight a frenzied rush. Already their full packs had become anchors on their shoulders, anchors slowing their flight from this park ranger dauntless in his tracking prowess. Their throats were parched as only the hunted can taste. On an inclined ledge the poachers decided to ditch their cargo of animal skins. They scrambled up the rocky knoll kicking the loose scree until they established a beachhead still within eyesight of their packs, but possessing the advantage of height now on their pursuer.

Salvador Maria Antonio sprinted after the poachers' trail aware of every step before it fell. He ran through the jungle silent, leaping over tuffs of grass, cruising through thick ferns, and even stepping ever-so-carefully on the turtle-backed rocks in the mud pools which would have given the casual observer the impression he indeed was walking on water. Deliberate with every step, he leapt through his park knowing full well what it was that he protected and the lengths to which he needed to go to accomplish his duty.

Corcovado National Park had been a nature preserve for over thirty years, which meant encroaching poachers who were now on their third generation of trespassing into land protected by the Costa Rican government. They operated with near impunity though, as the staffing levels at the ranger stations were filled with few rangers, and fewer still who either felt compelled to chase down the thieves or had the ability to do so. Their practice was cruel and quick; the ocelot jungle cat was baited, trapped, and skinned while the carcass was left to rot still attached to the bear-claw style steel trap. Naturally a thriving market demanding the skins encouraged the poachers to exact their villainy on these beautiful animals.

Salvador Maria Antonio showed an equal measure of compassion to the poachers as they did to their prey. His birth and youth in the jungle had honed a Tarzanian ability to use its strengths as his own; his amplified natural senses combined with an unyielding endurance made Salvador Maria Antonio the apex predator here, and the poachers knew it.

Their hearts pumped nervous with blood that seemed ready to burst arterial walls. Their breathing was dense and muffled as they reclined against the precipice overlooking the lush life-infused canopy below. It screamed its angst back at them. The shrill barbs of sound pierced their ears. Salty drops of sweat beaded on their collective brows. A nervous canteen of water was hurriedly passed amongst them. Their muscles ached. They hoped against reason that he would find some comfort in finding their backpacks and end his search there.

Not ones to typically find salvation in prayer, each of the three poachers removed a black steel rifle. The three positioned themselves sniper-style on the ridge triangulating on their packs. Carved with dynamic relief in their hilts, the rifles' cross-hairs fixed on the approaching ranger. Daylight scopes zoomed in on the position of their packs. The resulting image was clear enough to read the "Made in China" tag at this magnification. High caliber slugs designed to be molten upon impact were on tap at the firing pin. Safety releases were relaxed and the poachers prepared to bag their biggest prey yet.

Salvador Maria Antonio trusted the monkeys. Where they were to him was less important than where they weren't. High on the confines of the ledges above him he noticed the complete stillness of life even as he ran onwards along the poachers' trail. None of their curious monkey heads protruded from a characteristic perch overlooking the canopy, a clear indication to Salvador Maria Antonio that the poachers had holed up high above him. They had the advantage of height now. Ahead he immediately saw their packs.

He had given good chase, the paychecks of their weeklong killing spree were bundled in those massive packs. Given the bulk of the packs he suspected they had over a dozen pelts in each, a small fortune he immediately knew they wouldn't abandon so easily. As he bowled over the bend where they had left their packs Salvador Maria Antonio instinctively ran off the trail towards a bramble of blooming, concealing ferns.

"Kapow! Kapow! Kapow!" Three bursts of fire from the ledge above sounded.

For a moment Salvador Maria Antonio continued to run at his breakneck pace, but liquid fire surged through his back and thighs before the rapport of the gun fire ever crackled back to the poachers.

His body seized and fell into a roll. His limp frame plummeted to the earth sliding forcefully into a clutch of roots. Handle over tip, tip over handle, his machete clanged against the bumpy ground and fell silent next to him.

The jungle came alive with screaming capuchin monkeys and shrill, piercing jungle hens reacting to the shots. Their boisterous jeers fell through the clouds like rain, igniting a carnival atmosphere in the confines of a jungle swath. For a long while the noise was overwhelming, only ceasing to be deafening when the poachers finally eased off their perches and walked into the growth below. Tension returned to the jungle floor. The inhabitants watched expectantly as the poachers descended. It wasn't difficult to follow the blood spatter on the fern leaves. The poachers began to confirm their assumption that they indeed had picked-off Salvador Maria Antonio.

Red bandanas embroidered with an orange setting sun absorbed the beads of sweat on their brows. Corcovado had yet to have the afternoon rain so the air was stifling in the roots of the jungle. Moisture clumped together in the veins of ferns. In the distance, beyond the poachers' awareness, the sky ignited with light. At their feet thousands of industrious ants each carried more than his own weight in foliage back to the nest. The wiggling green line stretched as far as the eye could see. Stepping softly, each man circled around the ferns pooling water. Cautiously the poachers walked through the pleasant green foliage looking for red. Bright red.

A drop there, a splatter here, it didn't take them long to close in on Salvador Maria Antonio. Then they smelled it. A smooth, sweet caramel scent filled the air. It waffled delicately on their palates. The cigar's pleasantry took them all away for a moment to their own first tastes. It was so out of place in the jungle to smell the intoxicating air of a cigar burning away. The smoke filtered in and out of the light, obscured fully now by an enormous cashew tree looming ahead of the poachers.

Carved by the imagination of God, the cashew tree rose from the jungle floor to the height of heaven above, monopolizing all visible air rights with its canopy and sequestering any open ground as its own. Only a rough hewn path, jutting with rocks, welcomed them to the tree. Twice again the thickness of their outstretched arms, the cashew tree's trunk rose ominously above them. At its base lay a worn machete.

Weary eyes locked. The poachers drew their rifles up and clamored around the width of the giant cashew tree. Another whiff of the cigar filled the air. One of the poachers stayed back, while the other two crept around the left side of the tree following a crimson trail sprayed on the ferns. The sounds of strained breathing lumbered just beyond their sight. Two poachers wheeled around the tree keeping their rifles on point, one aimed high, the other low. Two shots blasted out, then silence.

"Do you have him?" The poacher who remained by the front of the tree yelled.

The sounds of tense struggle wrapped around the tree and into the jungle. Muffled groans and grunts succumbed finally to the sound of clanging rifles. The poacher in front of the tree ran towards his comrades. They lay lifeless on the ground with their red bandanas stuffed into their mouths. Breath imperceptible to the naked eye silently filled their lungs and pumped oxygen-starved blood, along with an unhealthy dose of poison tree frog, through their lungs. The lone standing poacher snapped his head around, but the machete lying on the mossy rocks had disappeared. A languishing cigar hung wrapped in a vine above his shoulders.

Where was the ranger? He swung his rifle around. No one was there. His knees shook together. He whirled around and fired.

Nothing.

He arched high at a shadow and fired.

Nothing.

He held the rifle poised on his hips circling the air trying to get a beat on the ranger. A crackle behind him sounded. The poacher spun around and fired three quick shots in the direction of a fallen cashew. Nothing.

The jungle went silent again, save for the "whoshing" sound of a helicopter. Only "whosh, whosh, whosh," pierced the jungle's silent abstraction before his scream.

The worn machete pierced through his thigh and firmly sunk into the cashew tree's trunk.

He was pinned. Pivoting instinctively with his rifle, the poacher aimed in slow motion for the animal rushing him. Salvador Maria Antonio unrolled from his tuck and sprang at the poacher. The firing pin struck. A lone bullet rifled down the steel barrel. The bullet cleared, then the smoke. Salvador Maria Antonio rushed forward and snatched away the rifle with his left hand as the bullet tore through the collar of his shirt. The ranger landed a solid right hook and left the poacher in an unconscious heap.

Salvador Maria Antonio stood with the weight of the jungle providing a laudable backdrop for its champion. Unscathed, save for an annoying flesh wound, he walked over to the vine and unraveled his cigar. Salvador Maria Antonio drew its amber tip back to life.

# PART THREE

▼

## LIFE'S LESSON

♠ ♥ ♣ ♦

THE FURNACE BLAZED. Specks of gold melted as the loose sand around them crackled. Congealing together, droplets joined each other and soon a little pool had formed in the crucible's concavity. The melting spread evenly now piecing all the intricate pieces of this elemental puzzle together.

Declan gazed at the bright orange mixture. He griped the crucible tightly. The broad lip of the crucible released the liquid fortune smoothly into his mold anchored on the workbench. Its bright orange hue would burn unprotected eyes. Declan's flame-resistant mittens lowered the crucible onto the workbench. He closed the furnace door and edged his protective mask open using his elbow.

In the seconds that followed, a thin black crust coated the mold as the most ductile and malleable metal on earth rapidly cooled. He doused the mold in water. It sputtered and hissed at him. Using the steel claws, Declan flipped the mold over and left it hovering just above the workbench softly tapping the mold with a rubber hammer. With a soft thud, the gold bar plopped down on the rubberized workbench.

Flashes of lightening and crackles of thunder signaled the afternoon's start. The morning's humidity now fell from the sky. Declan sat on a collapsible stool and watched the afternoon's tropical rain pelt the sidewalk outside. The cement building remained silent even as his neighbor's tin roofs crackled with the intensity of the downpour.

The furnace's fiery ruby eased to a smooth burgundy as it cooled. Warm vapor trails drifted upward from the magnificent bar lying motionless on the table. Declan went to the sink. He pulled off the fire-resistant cloak and slipped off his mitts. He hung them both on a bronze mermaid fashioned into a coat hanger.

Declan washed his hands. Caked soot dropped off his arms and made the bottom of the sink look like a carbon pit. A black liquid ring spiraled down the drain, chugging along the smooth porcelain into the pipes below. He dabbed his hands dry on his pants. Declan walked to the front of his business and let the gold bar cool unattended.

It didn't take an MBA, although Declan had one, to see that his business was booming. All twelve phone lines were occupied and another four calls, indicated by the flashing green lights, were on hold. Declan walked through the minimalist office and checked on the day's take so far.

It was a Friday afternoon, and already the offshore sports betting numbers looked spectacular. Friday evening usually went as late as 4 am, leaving Declan little time to rest. But it was like printing money, and probably the best thing going in Costa Rica for a small-time entrepreneur. His four years spent in Boston's Babson College entrepreneurial business program was far more than he needed. Without the requisite Boston political connections and having a total lack of blue blood, Declan sought his fortune elsewhere.

He had started his operations with a used 486 computer when he arrived in Costa Rica, but now the business had morphed into twelve full-time employees with another six part-time workers to help meet the unceasing demand by the North American clients he helped service sporting bets. A simple 1-800 number was his lifeline to the world. It connected his operation directly from San Jose, Costa Rica to the United States. With his entire staff bilingual and shift-based, Declan was able to capitalize on the fact that regardless of whether a client was in Boston or San Francisco, he was immediately able to make a bet. More importantly, far more importantly however, was the fulfillment of the transaction. Trust was a valuable commodity, a gambler once burned would never return, nor recommend the service to his compatriots.

With the introduction of high-speed internet access, mobile phones, and international electronic payment systems like PayPal, Declan was able to turn a backwater thousand square foot office he leased for $400 USD a month into a viable business growing in excess of 50% per annum. Last year it netted him just under two hundred thousand dollars.

Since much of 1-800-BET-ONIT's operation had become streamlined, and being first-to-market had established instant brand identity, Declan found that he could disappear for several weeks and monitor his operations by a global mobile phone even from the jungle he was exploring for gold. His secret to success was building a team of motivated employees and paying them five times the going Costa Rican salary rate. In addition, he subsidized all their housing expenses as well as provided liberal holiday policies. Plus he never reneged on a client's bet.

Make no doubt though, he was in the business of making money and was always trying to maximize this incredibly profitable niche business wholly condoned by the Costa Rican government. How else was Declan going to make replacement orders for the gear he had lost in his last foray into the jungle without a profitable business?

All the field equipment from his previous salvo was destroyed, better put, pulverized. He leaned over to work on his computer when a jagged pain shot through his leg. He looked down at the throbbing mass and knew it would still be a while until he would be well enough to make the trek back into the jungle. The antibiotics he was on helped, but the pain remained steadfast.

Declan sat down and flipped through the Tico Times, the premiere English newspaper in the country serving the needs of an ever-increasing gringo influx.

Most of the articles revolved around the political landscape, with brief pieces on eminent domain issues as well as a short story on the ramifications to the tax code of supplementing the universal health care system. Declan yawned. He flipped closer to the back of the magazine as his fingers acquired the classic black print smudges. And there in the third column of the last page something caught his eyes.

It seems a research group from the U.S. planned on launching a thorough archeological dig into Corcovado with particular emphasis on the Cerro Tigre heights, exactly where he had been investing all his exploration time. He threw the newspaper down in disgust. Without a second though, Declan picked up the phone and dialed his equipment supplier.

He was going to need more than standard scuba diving equipment to launch a foray into the jungle again. Previously, he had used traditional diving gear that had proven to be more difficult moving around the jungle than he had anticipated. Even with the custom sled he had designed, the bulky generator and full-piece harness ensemble was practically useless when he needed to be working in thick, steep, and even more remote regions. He would have to use either a smaller tank system or perhaps a compressor system that could float behind him.

The phone rang in Colorado Springs, CO of all places. Surprisingly, Colorado had become one of the epicenters for gold dredging, along with Alaska, where they designed custom systems for divers who traversed streams and riverbeds in search of granular gold.

The system Declan was most interested in was an open end filtration system that used gravitational spinning to quickly separate the good material, i.e. gold, from the sandy muck he often encountered in the pools in Costa Rica. The problem that usually arose after only several hours work, however, was that the gravity filtration system clogged with sandy muck. It was just too much work for such a fine filter. He really needed two filters, one rough and the other fine. The rough filtration could be performed in the water, while the fine filtration executed on shore would provide some flexibility. Staging the filtration process allowed Declan some much-needed down time to fully to process the site's riverbed sediment. Procuring the actual fluvial gold during an expedition was extremely time consuming from initial dredge to ultimate smelt.

Naturally both systems would have to be extremely efficient; compact, powerful, and as corrosion resistant as possible. The one man he trusted to design custom systems on the fly was Tucker Jones, a mechanical engineer of some renown who after serving in the Air Force for six years left and started his own machine shop.

Tucker worked with a variety of customers, from Department of Defense types to friends he had met in his travels around the world. Tucker was now immobilized due to a motorcycle accident several years ago on the torturous paths along the Rockies. His custom-designed "wheelchair" served as testament to his ability to construct the unimaginable from simple willpower.

"Tucker," he picked up the phone on the third ring and knew pretty much who it was by the latest phone identification tracking software he had developed. There was no such thing as "No Caller ID" for Tucker. He just grimaced wondering how much he owed on his sports betting tab and when Declan would indeed be rolling back into the office.

"Tucker you bum, says here your stub is over $20,000, what went wrong buddy?" Declan jabbed while inhaling a swath of cigar smoke billowing in his private office.

"Declan! My man, it's been a while! Glad to hear you're back in town. Heard some rumblings things didn't go quite as planned for you on the last expedition." Tucker smirked back.

His IT system in Colorado Springs was top-notch to say the least, providing him with preprogrammed information RSS feeds on a rule set he developed that helped track the status of both his friends and it goes without saying his not-so-friends. More than a news feed service, the VirtuThere™ system provided geographic information harnessing the latest overhead satellite resources he could plug into. Granted, it proved to be a difficult task to check up on friend when there was foliage covering his every move, but Tucker helped get around this problem with the aid of some nanotechnology he had developed and inserted into many of the products he sold. MiniBeacons™ were GPS transmitters that harnessed ambient temperature differentials to electrically charge themselves and transmit on randomly generated times their locations.

"Tucker, as usual you know too much. Too bad your betting prowess isn't as keen, otherwise I'd really have a problem! Now listen bud, in return for your balance I need a little work done on designing some custom gear for a trip back into the jungle. The last expedition proved to be a bit too arduous…if at all possible I'd like to regroup in the not-to-distant future and make my way back to a site." Declan finished his words and chomped back down on his cigar.

"El Tigre, I assume?" Tucker eyed the phoned knowing full well where Declan planned to dredge next.

"Indeed my friend, El Tigre it is. Seems like I need to make a jump on it as well, because the Tico Times just published a feature about an archeological team heading down to my area soon. Obviously I'd like to conduct my exploration and mining without having to deal with a Costa Rican sanctioned research vessel breathing down my neck. Bad enough, I have to lug all this gear in and out, but I can do quite well without a team of archeologists running around the place. Check your email."

Declan palmed his phone, opened his private office door, and walked into the smelting lab. His bar of gold remained caked in soot on the workbench. He picked up a coarse towel and while holding the phone against his shoulder rubbed the gold bar down. Black carbon chunks fell off the bar and onto the table. He brought the pure gold bar up to a dull luster with yet another cloth as they continued their conversation.

"Alright Declan, let's see what we have here," Tucker read the email had just received from Declan. Imbedded in it he found a list of instructions on exactly what Declan wanted designed. His eyes shot back and forth over his screen and examined all the potential ways to design the system.

"Declan, this is going to take a little more than my balance to design, construct, and deliver to you. Heck delivery now eats up nearly 20% of the cost." Tucker nervously tapped his keyboard.

"I figured you'd say that. I'm sending up a small sample of what I've been able to pull out over the weeks working this site. Should cover your curiosity expenses and give you a little something to smile about, everybody loves a little golden sunshine in their lives." Declan grinned and cupped the kilo bar in his hands.

♠ ♥ ♣ ♦

PULL. PULL. PULL. Inside the cylinder air mixed with gasoline then sparked to life. Puttering smoke cleared and the engine droned on faintly.

Declan pushed the floating dredge along the narrow river inlet until it was positioned on a shallow bank. The river's water was tepid due to the mix of saltwater coming in from the ocean waves and the draining water empting in from the hills above. On each bank scattered driftwood mingled with fingernail-sized pebbles layered the foreground to an immense jungle backdrop. The lush, tangled, impenetrable greenery rose over the hills and receded only on the steepest inclines to reveal jagged stone ledges.

Life was everywhere. Scarlet macaws screeched along the fringe separating the jungle from the ocean. Brown volcanic earth transitioned the ground from the heights of the jungle to the beach surf. Dividing all of this was a riverbed some eighty feet wide at the mouth that constricted to the width of single kayak as it entered the jungle.

Loose sediment from high in the jungle hills above fell into the river's current where it was whisked downstream into pools and shallow deltas no deeper than a man's waist. This is where Declan plunged into the water with his half-wetsuit, sneakers, and mask to dredge the rich mineral deposits.

The ten-foot long tubes with a diameter of four inches sucked up all the underwater sand, swirled the dirty mixture into gravity filters and ultimately exuded the debris out the back end. The gravity filter quickly separated matter with the greatest density, keeping the desired heavy particulate and passing the rest. It was tedious, heavy work. Manual labor at its most unrefined. Indeed, when Declan finally took the time one day to divide the hours worked by the wholesale gold price he would receive, it had yet to pay minimum wage. Nonetheless, the adventurer in him dredged onward hoping to score a rich vein of fluvial gold.

For the stretch of a week or more Declan would dredge an area before returning back to base camp to recoup. His time in the sun combined with the constant exposure to the saltwater had turned his skin a dark olive tone, which contrasted quite nicely with his aqueous eyes so full of light. He was as far away from being a fluorescent light indentured office worker shackled to personal computer as possible. Declan was physically fit and mentally sharp, he embodied the masculine pura vita that defined the jungles of Costa Rica themselves.

Disappointment, though, always seemed to rear its ugly head. Time after time Declan had found an exciting river inlet to prospect only to be disappointed with the results. On this occasion, however, during his site survey he noticed that the mouth of the river met the ocean and the resulting formation resembled an hourglass. Where the thick upper section of the river compressed, then widened to the ocean head, a deep fissure clearly jutted into the ground. Taking his mask to the water's surface, he took a peek underwater. Declan saw an underwater cavern. It begged to be explored.

He pulled the dredging equipment on the sandy bank, anchoring it high enough to survive any sudden water spike, and proceeded to flip through the gear he needed to make an initial dive into the fissure.

The fissure seemed surprisingly deep considering its proximity to shore. Declan took his pony bottle with him. It was a miniature scuba tank; 13 cubic feet of air compressed at 3000 lbs. per square inch into the size of a 2-litre Coke bottle. It seemed so cute and innocent, but he knew that even this baby bottle of air was essentially equivalent to a small missile if the main value ever failed.

He strapped the pony bottle in a self-designed Velcro arm band which served to secure the tank to his right biceps. A regulator wound up from the top of the pony bottle, its hose proved to be the perfect length to his jaw.

Declan keep his half wetsuit on, dubbed a "shorty," as well as his weight belt and strapped on his lower left calf a dive knife. Not that he was expecting any trouble, the knife in fact had a square head more useful for prying samples than for any possible defensive maneuver. So along with his mask, short fins, a small mesh catch bag and a thin light looped to his wrist Declan prodded along the shore of the river until he was parallel to the fissure and eased in the water.

He opened the valve of the pony bottle and heard the distinctive sound of compressed air rushing to fill the regulator's hose. Declan took two deep safety breaths to check the regulator's flow and then immediately slipped below the surface.

The current at the cusp of the fissure was firm, and it took his powerful legs several seconds to stabilize before he could steady himself at the cavern's entrance. At once though, he fell through the fissure's tight spigot of an entrance and immediately descended. The previously intense current completely evaporated below the cusp of the cavern.

Compressed air bubbled at the surface. Declan sucked in deep full breaths of the compressed jungle air as he scanned the contours of this underwater cavern.

He was overwhelmed. Along the riverbeds he occasionally found small inlets that dropped away from the upper crusted lip of the riverbank, but never anything like this.

Declan had once swam against a current up to a natural waterfall. Diving near a waterfall often had its own challenges, like never knowing what was going to come over the crest. Entering this cavern, however, was the most challenging endeavor. Already Declan could tell, this was far larger and more complex than his initial survey had predicted. He focused his mind on the task at hand and pushed aside his numerous other forays into the water. For now his mind was occupied only with exploring this cavern.

Its depth and breadth were difficult for him to discern as he only had his back-up flashlight as the primary light source. The brilliant, but narrow, beam sliced across the cavern's stillness.

The water became noticeably warmer as he swam in further, and the further he swam in the more difficult he found it to turn. The current had shifted and each fin kick propelled him deeper into a dark abyss.

Declan looked at his pressure gauge to check on the amount of air remaining. He noticed his consumption rate had spiked, his eyes quickly zeroed in on the depth gauge. He was sinking! In the brief interlude since his entrance into the cave he had descended from a shallow fifteen feet to well over fifty. The cavern was a massive hollow pocket under the river! He considered the possibility of a lava burst hundreds, if not thousands of years ago, had formed a shelf allowing both for a surface river as well as a fully housed cavern. Declan descended further into the cavern. The water continued to feel warmer by the foot, uncomfortably so now. His flashlight finally registered a bottom, a bottom with shifting sands. Declan eased his descent as best he could.

His narrow beam of light helped illuminate the cavern's darkness. His eyes tried to read the blurry contours of the fissure. It became immediately obvious that this cavern was far more complicated than he had every expected.

"National Geographic is going to love this," Declan thought.

For one, the cavern's depth surpassed the vertical range of his flashlight. That meant the cavern was in excess of eighty feet, the typical Costa Rican ocean visibility conditions. Secondly, he found himself no longer alone, but rather in the sullen company, towards his rear naturally, of a handsome and impeccably dressed quartet of bull sharks who seemed to be sleeping just below the lip of the fissure. Bulls had the distinct advantage in the shark family of a gill structure that allowed them to survive not only in the temperate seawater, but also in brackish water and fresh water. Suddenly Declan realized why he had sunk so quickly, he had assumed his lead would be used in salt water to counteract his natural buoyancy. In fresh water he was actually negative!

Coming out without disturbing the bulls already posed a challenge, a challenge Declan suspected he would rather have had a pointed knife or better yet some sort of excessively long pointed pole to deal with; a bang-stick wouldn't be bad either.

With a cautious eye leering back at his compatriots in the cavern, Declan proceeded to ease his way gradually deeper to the fissure bottom. He had gone this far and wasn't quite ready to turn around just yet. The cavern walls upon closer inspection were not of the limestone deposits he so frequently encountered, but rather were indeed volcanic rock. It was as if he had entered into a massive lava tube.

Coarse ripples of long-cooled magma made seemingly straight lines contort with the light of a flashlight upon them. Their imbued obsidian specs canvassed the whole of the fissure. They writhed like black cobras along the floor of some forbidden temple.

Declan finally reached the far end of the cave, some one hundred and twenty fin kicks from the entrance. And it was there, where he motioned to make his return along the same path, that something caught his eye.

It was deeper still than his present depth, perhaps another twenty feet down. But there, amongst some rich earth fully absorbed his flashlight's beam came the dizzying reflection, rather a sharp and immediate tinge, of gold pixels.

Declan eased his breathing, arched his back, and motioned to descend.

Suddenly his side burst into pain, an immense biting pain. He recoiled instantly into a cloud of his own blood that had darkened the water about him. Then it was his arm, torn off nearly it felt like. The pony bottle ripped off its Velcro fastener and his regulator gone just as fast. His right hand instinctively grabbed the buckle of his weight belt and let the lead fall. He began to ascend rapidly in the cavern.

He kept his wits, gritted his teeth, and purposely exhaled as he kicked up. Declan smashed hard against the ceiling of the cave. Fortunately, the cave had collected a pool of his exhausted air. Declan gasped deeply of this pocket of precious gas and peered below through a cracked mask lens. The bulls circled in a wild rodeo below, frenzied with the pleasure of meat in their chops and the scent of blood prodding them onward, and dangerously, upward.

They bolted up toward Declan's legs in an attempt to pull him down. Declan curled into a muscular ball while rotating 180 degrees, grabbed his chiseling tool, and sprang headfirst into their jaws. In an instant he narrowly dodged one's gaping mouth only to clumsily stab at the other beast and drop the knife.

It wasn't without merit though. The bull shark's eye socket had been torn with the blow and along with it a heady chuck of the bull's leathery skin also stood agape. Not a mortal wound by any means, but agape enough for the other bulls to take notice.

Declan spun around and torpedoed towards the opening to the fissure. His mask was filling with water.

He kicked wildly without regard to the efficiency of his kicks, but rather a mad foray towards a dim natural light he saw swathed in the distance. So distant.

He kicked hard, but came upon the conclusion that he was going to run out of air long before he could make his escape.

"Shallow water drowning," he agonized, "all my time diving, in all the places in the world, and I'm going to die fifteen feet underwater!"

His lungs screamed, but there was no air to be had. It constricted his movements and he felt the anguish of near success creep along the worn, weary, and weathered contours of his frame.

At once a bull bit through his fin and flipped Declan upside down dragging him along the narrowing contours of the fissure bumping his torso, with a great chunk of his wetsuit missing, along the bottom of the jagged volcanic rock. A thousand knives drew their blades on him.

The unmistakable fluorescent yellow of his pony bottle smacked him in the head as the bull drug him back. It was nearly within his reach. Nearly. He jerked his leg free, leaving the fin in the bull's jaws and desperately shot out his arm toward the pony bottle prize. The aluminum wiggled just out of his grasp.

"Air!" his mind screamed silently.

The current pushed him forward. Throbbing fingers made one final grab. He had it! The regulator was gone, but no matter. He anchored the bottle with one fell swoop using his armpit and opened the tank full tilt. Cupping his hands, funneled the air to his mouth.

The dry air shot up to his mouth along with an unhealthy dose of salt water. He inhaled it all. Two deep breaths, that's all Declan needed, and that's all he got. He kicked towards the cavern's mouth and saw a pair of bulls blocking his escape.

Declan took the pony bottle by the neck valve and thrust in into the head of the closer bull leaving the valve open full-tilt to aerate the entire opening of the fissure. It worked. The bulls dashed apart and left the opening clear.

He shot out of the cavern and into the tumultuous current. It whipped him away from the fissure directly out to sea. Declan jack-knifed his body around and clawed his way to the rocky beach, any port in this storm would do.

He flopped on the cobbled rock and clamored ashore. Declan stumbled momentarily, regained his footing, and pressed forward to the safety of higher ground. The bulls couldn't come ashore, but the crocodiles had scent enough of his injuries to press their case. He lumbered up the terrace of the jungle, pushing forward pained steps not even realizing he had one fin still on and his mask had formed a dark ring around his face. Finally Declan collapsed.

He had made it to the outer fringe of the jungle, high and deep enough along the elevated root structure to virtually guarantee his safety. Jagged shards of rock encrusted with thick clumps of gold filled his mess bag and pressed softly again his shredded skin. The jungle diver ceased breathing.

♠ ♥ ♣ ♦

SHE KNELT ABOVE him with a worried look taking full stock of his battered body still oozing blood from the underwater cavern. His head rolled to the side and she saw his latest request for gear slumped over on the beach sand beside him. Declan moaned softly and opened his eyes.

Swollen hands clung to her soft skin freckled by Irish birth and tanned by the Costa Rican sun. Lauren felt his pulse and sighed. It was weak, but at least better than when she had found him strewn in the underbrush. Declan motioned to stand, but could barely sit-up. He was battered and fully beaten. His brow was split and his knees shredded. Hermit crabs feasted on the raw meat hanging off his legs. Lauren laid his head down gently.

She peered across the inlet to where several of his gear bags lay. Swiftly she ran over to the other shore, grabbed the bag with clothes, and left the rest. She tore the t-shirts into wraps and administered first responder medical aid to Declan after removing what remained of his wetsuit with a pointless dive knife slopped on the beach. Immediately Lauren went out to the clearest point and radioed ahead to the Sirena Ranger Station. She knew Salvador Maria Antonio was in the park this month.

The radio crackled static, then went silent. She was out of range. Lauren looked at him as she considered her options.

His chin pointed up with unshorn bristles buckling out while a strong nose peered her directly in the eyes. His breathing had stabilized after being too shallow for her comfort. His frame was wholly lean and fully muscular, and battered. Years of scars indicated that injury was definitely a lifelong companion of his. Even one of his calves looked strikingly smaller than the other.

Lauren reached in his bag looking for something that could be a resource to help get him out of here. Her hand felt a metal tube. Sweeping a pair of sweatpants away, Lauren discovered a flare gun. Her mind came alive. She reached into the pack and removed the gun. It was a Matador 2000 flare gun, a marine flare gun used by commercial fisherman for distress in unimaginable circumstances miles off the coast or in even the heaviest weather. It was plenty strong to catch the eye of the ranger station some twelve miles away.

Lauren stepped forward and pointed the gun in the air. Her finger squeezed the trigger just as she felt his hand wrap around her ankle and his voice moan "No..."

It was too late to stop. The flare shot out of its tube, but Lauren had flinched when Declan grabbed her ankle. The flare lobbed in a low arc over the sandy shore. The flare hit the water, skipped along the wave tops, and detonated under the water just far enough away for them to hear a little "poof." A waft of New Year's fireworks filled the air briefly and the jungle listed about noiselessly as it always does at noon.

Lauren spun around and reached for Declan. "Why did you do that?"

Declan loosened his grip on her ankle. Painfully he rolled on his side. "The ranger station...I shouldn't...be here..." His speech was raspy, broken, a struggling wind of virtually incomprehensible noise.

Lauren stepped back. Her amber locks jingled around as she pulled her ankle free from his grip. He lay motionless on the ground save for his lungs' struggle to breath. His chest looked like several ribs had been broken, bruised indents checkered his torso. Lauren knelt cautiously. "Can you hear me?" She stroked his hair softly.

Declan moaned and looked up at her as if he'd just woken up from a dream that lasted hours, but past singularly in a moment. "Where... am...I?" Declan pivoted his head towards Lauren and filled his eyes full of her. Angelic in her motions she seemed lighter than air.

"Are...you...an angel?" Declan crunched his abdomen forward as shocks of pain overcame him and stole a kiss. He fell back on the sand, comatose.

♠ ♥ ♣ ♦

DECLAN USED HIS heels to rub up against the sand and push his way up along a palm tree. "Where was she?" He wondered. Lauren tumbled down an inlet trail emerging from the jungle with a full canteen of water and seemingly pleased with herself. His radio was strapped along her waist.

"No, against my better judgment, I didn't put a radio call through," Lauren eyed him with her words before the question came on his lips.

"Many thanks…seems like I'm digging myself deeper and deeper into owing you favors before we've even formally met." Declan smiled. He had regained some color in his cheeks and was surprisingly in quite good spirits. He sat in the shade with a blanket draped over him and his wounds dressed neatly, expertly. Declan motioned to stand.

"Sit." Lauren snapped at him like he was a disobedient pup, which in all truthfulness he was.

Gallantry aside, Declan remained seated but extended his weathered hand out to her silky one. "Declan Mares, and rest assured, I am very pleased to meet you." The gleam in his eye was more than just a squint from the setting sun.

"Declan…somehow I've heard that name before. You wouldn't have happened to have run into Ranger Salvador Maria Antonio in the park before would you? Something about dredging for gold?"

49

Lauren let her eyes follow the contours of the sand leading up to his outstretched hand.

"It was more of a geological survey, so to speak." Declan grimaced and held her hand firmly as they shook.

"Lauren McAlister, PhD candidate and Corcovado aficionado." She smiled.

"Hmmm…that rhymes Miss, I assume Miss, McAlister?" Declan pressed.

"Ms." Lauren eyed him playfully.

"So what brings you into this neck of the woods?" With the emphasis on the word "neck" Declan let his mind wander. The sun was well on its way to setting and the scene before him was majestic.

Ripples of water danced over the rough white surf and a halo of amber coated the coast. He hesitated to blink for fear of missing it all. So beautiful. So pure. His spirit calmed and he looked up at Lauren who was shaking her head in amusement.

"Mr. Mares, quite the Casanova aren't we? I study butterflies, a leapodiotrist for an educated man of which I'm not sure you are quite yet, and this park has become a second home to me over the years. The Sirena Ranger Station actually is home away from home." Lauren too felt the shift from day to evening begin to overcome the land.

Declan was too injured to transport, she knew that when she radioed the station telling them to expect her in the morning as she was planning to make camp on the shore. She slung off her backpack and let the driftwood that filled it tumble onto the sand. "I'll shore up some stones for a fire ring. Anything else I can get for you?"

"A cold beer and juicy steak, with a healthy side of potatoes would fit just nicely." Declan shot back smartly. He crawled over to the wood and began shucking the driftwood into usable pieces of firewood.

Lauren walked to the shoreline and back several times depositing with him several smooth, sea stones each time. In a matter of minutes together they had built an impressive fire ring with ample store of driftwood for the evening. As the last of day's light passed by them, a warm blaze illuminated their silhouettes against the darkening sky. A handful of stars sprinkled the early evening sky.

THE DAY-TRIPPERS ZIPPED along the surface of the sea watching the resort fade from view and the overwhelming presence of jungle envelop their horizon. They huddled tightly together. Mist soon turned to rain, rain that was strangely warm for visitors unaccustomed to the tropics. It pelted their exposed legs and forearms like little needles as the boat accelerated out of the bay and onto open ocean. The waves were full here. Deep, discerning waves that at points swallowed the boat whole then spat it up on the next peak. Their troughs were longer rather than deep though, which made the ride more fun than scary.

A guide, boat captain, and six tourists buzzed along the contours of the coast for the better part of an hour at which point it faded from view. Obscured by a thick fog, the coast effectively vanished. The only discerning landmark was visible as the black pixels on a handheld GPS. So they motored along in the gray soup of a day, weary of the thoughts of where they were in this water in reference to the actual coastline. Cheery faces succumbed to the monotonous rise and fall of the waves which lulled them all into a complacent silence. The engine's drone seemingly softened as they pulled into a clutch of snappy waves.

They moved headlong into the heart of Corcovado where the Sirena Ranger Station acted as headquarters. The station was constructed with a corrugated tin roof and gangly-green wood sections hammered together into a lodge capable of housing up to sixty researchers and their research equipment. An unimproved landing strip machete-hacked out of the jungle two thousand feet long and continually overgrown served as the most direct method of getting to the station. Given the fact that fog routinely blanked the station in a dark shroud, however, it proved difficult even for the most daring bush pilots to chance a landing. As the saying goes, there were old pilots and bold pilots but no old bold pilots. Without a doubt, Sirena's location served as the last bastion of civilization before the jungle fully consumed every trace of humanity.

The coastline was raw. Strewn with seeds as big as a human skull, driftwood, and clumps of limestone coral thick and bulby it projected a feeling of isolation. The tourists emerged from the warm rain cold and approached the shoreline at the only acceptable speed to overcome the surf; breakneck, with the captain's hand fully extended on the throttle. They were instructed to hold fast and they did, never a good position to fish out a client in swells frequently occupied with strong eddies and stronger bull sharks. The water slapped loudly against the vessel's hull.

"Smack, smash, bang!"

Hurtling flows from heavy surf shook everyone violently. This was no day trip for the faint of heart. Everyone was one their toes now.

"We're going to take it in quickly, make sure you have your sandals on now," the guide positioned the clients alongside the boat's rafters waiting for the right moment when the waves eased out and left the tourists in thigh-high water.

"OK, go for it, everyone in and get quick to shore, I'll bring up the gear."

The guide was a powerful man, thick in the chest and owning a particularly dark in complexion beyond a weathered tan or ethnical skin tone, but rather one infused with the shadows of the jungle. His hands grabbed gear instinctively for everyone in a massive lurching motion. He dipped into the thigh-high water that came up to his chest. He managed to easy hold all the gear for all seven safely above the water line and walk across the limestone rock checkered with volcanic impasses easily knowing when and where to step at all times.

The boat captain circled once and waived an adios, he headed out of the violent surf past the breakers. He sought the calm of a nearby peninsula whose landmass and sidelines of deep water offered some barrier protection for the boat.

The guide handed his clients their respective bags of gear. The rain had yet to let up, but as they entered the cover of the lush canopy it became dry once again for them.

Roots, vines, and leaves all vied to climb high and grab as much of the air space as possible, providing them with a natural umbrella whose few holes let little water pass. The guide swiftly changed from wearing nothing on his feet to thick wool socks and classic rubber boots tall past his knees. As each client put on expensive hiking boots or trekking sneakers fresh from REI, the guide smiled smugly and lassoed up his gear, mainly consisting of a high-powered telescopic viewing lens, with stand, and a small ruck sack. They pressed forward into the jungle with the rain softening the sound of their steps.

The trail, unperceivable save to the guide, winded forward and switched back as they ascended in elevation and came ultimately to a sloping ridgeline overlooking their drop-off point. From here the relief was dramatic. It was a window on this jungle world, offering a deep gaze into the confines of Corcovado. The view was filled with a wholesome, physical lushness. Their eyes succumbed to a voluptuous stare into the richness of flora and fauna Corcovado offered. The guide motioned above, placing his finger on his lips, and pointing off in the distance to an unrecognizable brown mound in the trees high above. At once his telescopic lens was positioned neatly on the little creature.

A sloth hung motionless, inanimate from the tree appearing to be nothing more than a gigantic fur ball superglued to the trunk of a true. A piercing scream high and to the right startled the group. Another. Then yet another. A troupe of howlers had happened upon them. Their dark shadows moved briskly between trees. Only the sight of a shaking branch here or fruit falling from there alerted the group to where the monkeys had gone. They seemed so fast, but perhaps all the humans were just utterly slow.

Each of the tourists had silently noticed a change about themselves as they entered deeper into the heart of the jungle. It was transformative, a calming presence that alleviated the construed pressures of the modern world around them. A burden of humanity slipped off each of their respective shoulders leaving them truly empowered, but more importantly aware. Aware of the true beauty, the beauty of nature that had encapsulated their previous self-awareness and now released them free again upon the world.

The guide motioned forward as each tourist entered Corcovado for the simply the first time. Their suctioning steps resonated amongst the group and their ability to see past the foliage and into the distance increased dramatically in the simple course of an hour. Shapes and forms previously unseen became obvious. Their nervous chatter so typical of the early morning departure had subsided into "oohs" and "ahhs," and finally they became reflective. They now saw Corcovado for what it was, a living, breathing sanctuary of life. It was truly a gift from God's own hand, unable to be replicated or replaced.

Ahead of the group, the guide had stationed his tripod and reached off the trail. He held cupped in his hand a string of bright red bulbs, circular-shaped with thin curling stalks emanating from every direction. Smiling he motioned the group forward.

"Is good," he tore off half the fruit's soft shell to reveal a translucent, fleshly bulb. He passed around a rambutan to each of the tourists. They did likewise and suctioned off the fruit from its casing and spat out the center seed after enjoying the crisp, sweet flesh.

The guide picked up his tripod and walked again down the trail. He stopped along the way here and there to point out particular features of the vegetation. Each fern, vine, and jutting outgrowth had a story, a use, and a purpose. For nearly five hours they walked in the jungle examining the flora, tasting her fruits, and experiencing what Corcovado meant.

For some it felt like a lifetime by the time they emerged from the jungle along the shore, for others it felt like just minutes. The guide had seen this every time a group had departed from the lodge and spent several hours simply walking in Corcovado. They were reflective now, borderline brooding, asking themselves in their hearts what they could do to keep this paradise their own secret forever. From the callous to the protective, each instinctively knew that their piece of this world would not fall victim to the modernization of the world surrounding it.

♠ ♥ ♣ ♦

Salvador Maria Antonio drove a drab, olive green Jeep. The vintage machine was long-ago removed from the confines of urban chic and transformed into a jungle shuttle. He sped around roads engulfed with stagnant eddies of muddy water.

They never seemed to evaporate. Pools of water simply languished, in one location or another, indefinitely. Just when the scorching midday sun had made some progress, afternoon showers refilled all the potholes. Most of them were only ankle deep, but occasionally one would consume an entire vehicle. They were born from the matrimony of poor road construction and the frequency of heavy rains. Without meaningful substrate under the single layer of concrete the road quickly developed these hollow traps. Salvador Maria Antonio shuffled his eyes restlessly around the contours of each shadow that had grown along his turns. He kept a watchful eye out for any small reflective pools. As the sun slipped below the tree line they turned darker still, like a chameleon blending into night.

Brambles of ferns and vines wrangled along the roadway. They traversed the rudimentary pavement Salvador Maria Antonio drove along toward the lodge. As he drove further he came upon a variation in the road. He could feel it from the sensation in the steeling wheel vibrating against his wrists. The pavement here was cut in large rectangular posts. They had been set along the approach to bridges.

By posting the blocks of concrete the engineers were able to secure the taunt steel suspension supports. Salvador Maria Antonio buckled over the bridge, slowing merely to gaze across the lush expanse below him.

The panoramic greenery stretched as far as he could see. Its contours fell long and deep into the early night, cloaking the eyes in a mist of green fog. The water running in the valley three hundred feet below arched over a bottleneck ledge until it burst into the air. The foamy water seemed to float as it fell, hovering there in a magical trance. Airy bubbles sprinkled and burst in the air, catching a thermal rush and floating high into the sky. The water below continued fast and furious into an ever-deepening gorge that had sequestered a number of smaller tributary waterfalls along the stretch of its path. The water brooded high on the hills and rushed full out after the afternoon rains. It sped through the natural earthen capillaries in the thick volcanic earth progressively gathering momentum as the water barreled home.

He drove along the edge of the grappling steel suspension bridge. Here, anchored by the massive concrete blocks, ferns clung to life against the sectioned-off soil. They hung precariously above the swift water. It was tough living for the ferns. They were a testament to nature's resolve, collecting enough soil piecemeal to propagate an entire carpet. The green throw-rugs dotted the sheer sides of the gorge like some camouflage patch-work quilt. Burrowing into the hills carpenter ants built massive nests that anchored the soil substrate and plant roots to the vertical rises and gave the walls an uncanny strength as some sort of natural adhesive gluing the earth, vegetation, and animal into one force.

Salvador Maria Antonio continued over the bridge and scanned the horizon. Already the fruit bats had started to hunt. A troop of capuchin monkeys had secured their evening resting place in a flowering hardwood, which given the buzzing presence about it, left him with the impression that the monkeys might not make a night of it if the bees' hive was disturbed. He down-shifted his Jeep as the road narrowed into nothing more than a loosely cut dirt lane angling left and right with vine roots shooting up and across the roadway. The night's coolness enveloped him and he thought it a proper time to pull on the headlights. He pulled the toggle and lit up the path with dry yellow beams. They only illuminated fifteen feet ahead of him in two narrow cones and did not go any further. Salvador pushed along the road further and finally drove out to the sea again.

In the distance he spied the ocean, it had settled in the evening from the afternoon rush and appeared to be entering its own placid retreat. Salvador Maria Antonio eased his foot off the clutch and put the Jeep into the third gear. It took the gear and speed through the defined dirt road that emerged.

Salvador Maria Antonio felt relief, mental and physical, knowing he would soon be back at the lodge. His body hurt all over after rounding up the smugglers. Already he knew their leaders were aware something had gone awry. Years ago it would have taken them months to redouble their efforts; he would be surprised it took longer than several days to outfit another group willing to take its chances along the path of their compadres.

The Jeep bounced along the final stretch of the dirt road that ended at the foot of a neglected dirt runway overgrown a month and needing his attention. Salvador Maria Antonio killed the engine. He hooked his rings of keys to a strap on his waist and tucked the strapped keys into a stitched pocket on his pants. He untied his backpack from the Jeep's crossbar and leaning against the vehicle slipped off his left boot, then his right, and walked barefoot to the lodge across a dirt path.

Softly in the distance he could hear a folk song playing and the distinct smell of coffee floated in the air. It was followed by grilling meat, definitely beef he thought, and the lodge's lights illuminating the path ahead of him. Salvador Maria Antonio stopped at the wash station and placed his things on the hardwood bench he had crafted from fallen giants, and turned on the free-standing faucet.

Overhead a shower gurgled to life. Warmed by the day's sun, it released a refreshing spray of fresh water that had been condensed from a salt-water bastion.

Salvador Maria Antonio grabbed the little liquid squirt bottle, washed his clothes while they were on his body, and then stripped. Quickly he placed the clothes in a plastic drum and washed them with the fresh water, rinsing them twice, wringing them dry, and then rinsing them a final time. He placed the drum aside and finished his shower.

He looked up at the water tank. Not bad, he thought, maybe ten gallons used. He patted himself dry with the fresh towel in the locker by the lodge's rear entrance. He swung it around his waist, picked up his gear and grabbed his clothes in the drum. He wrung them again and brought them with him into the station.

"Salvador," the station cook looked up at him, "glad to see you back here in one piece. That was some business you got into this afternoon."

"Manuel theses poachers are getting worse and worse," Salvador Maria Antonio tossed over the backpack slung over this shoulder and let it hit the kitchen floor with a thump. "Three of them today, all with rifles and they are just the ordinary skin and poach runners. The time will come when someone, something, more dangerous will come. Somehow they are drawn here." He thought about his last sentence, picked out a cigar from his vest and lit it.

Sweet smoke curled around Salvador Maria Antonio's lips.

"That is not true," Salvador Maria Antonio continued answering his own rhetorical question with a knowing nod. "They are drawn here for the same reason the tourists are drawn here, for the same reasons the explorers where drawn here, for the same reason the banana farmers were drawn here. The resources are in the ground. In the dirt. In the air. In the water. Everywhere we turn in the park there is something of tremendous value to someone."

Manuel shrugged. "They will keep coming Salvador. They will keep coming and coming. Every year there are more. Imagine the situation if the government hadn't made this a national park? The trees would have long ago been pulled from the earth. And the soil tilled and planted. Then burned, and then planted again until there was nothing left to pull from the soil."

Manuel stopped talking and opened the grill. Six steaks, twice again the size of a man's palm were cross-marked. A dozen ears of corn rolled over when he flipped their shells. On the stove a big vat of beans bubbled, and on the porch with the swinging lanterns a coffee pot dripped.

"Sustainable Salvador," Manuel continued, "is not enough. We need to dissuade."

Salvador Maria Antonio smiled. Manuel's reasoning was sound, but he knew this ranger station didn't support itself. Indeed, until Corcovado became a National Park there were no funds for a unit of rangers, never mind a well-outfitted station. The constant stream of tourists had infused the country with meaningful dollars. Dollars, Euros, and Yen for that matter. Massive infusions of foreign currency that came packed along with the digital video cameras, binoculars, and tubes of bug repellent. He could deal with the marauding poachers and even the itinerant prospector. That concerned him, but it didn't keep him up at night worrying. What kept him up at night worrying was in a vial in his backpack. A vial filled with a black, viscous, hydrocarbon.

# PART FOUR

▼

# LIFE'S WORTH

♠ ♥ ♣ ♦

She was a sleek vessel with all of the latest technology embedded in her. Composite AlumoGraf™ structure, high-speed everything; mobile internet, fuel compression, GPS, and a crew team of long-distance racers. IPEEC spared no expense in designing and outfitting the *Modern Explorer* for her various forays into some of the most inhospitable place on earth. They couldn't afford not to, the stakes in the global hunt for oil were too high.

The first renditions of the petroleum giants' vessels were lumbering steel masses that beckoned for Greenpeace action. Unsightly and willfully cavalier, these early boats bemoaned indecency. By the late eighties, however, a new breed of boat had surfaced that had proven to be an exceptional choice for explorations in either shallow or choppy water, or both. The ship was designed with durability, workability, and comfort in mind.

*Modern Explorer* was a massive catamaran approaching two hundred feet long and outfitted with an onboard reverse osmosis water system capable of diffusing five thousand gallons a day of seawater into clean, crisp drinking water. Naturally, an onboard assay laboratory came standard issue along with some of the fastest mobile communications systems in the world. *Modern Explorer* could batch assay test several thousand samples a day, crunch the data, build the relevant models, and then beam the results back home all in a day's work.

Bobbing softly in the sun's rising light, she stood ready to sail. The vessel had been fully outfitted in the Port of Houston, a vibrant epicenter of waterborne tonnage and a petro job center. The Port of Houston alone created nearly 800,000 jobs and generated over $100 billion economic impact to Texas. The hot, hazy disguise encapsulating the port proved to be a perfect cloak to as *Modern Explorer* sailed through Galveston Bay. *Modern Explorer* would be engine tested across the Gulf of Mexico to southern Florida. The full crew compliment along with the research scientists, engineers, and field sample collectors would board in Key West. From there they would blast south through the Panama canal and over to the Pacific side of Costa Rica. Already the various crew components had carved out their respective dens on board and looked eager to push off.

*Modern Explorer* motored into its temporary home for the coming months, anchoring just a long swim away from the entrance of Corcovado National Park. The hull was a bright white topical paint, a blinding oddity in a wilderness canvassed in olive. Famished for being at sea so long, the crew made quick time readying the vessel and pushed headlong in no time towards the shore in one of the two small power boats.

It buzzed along the crests of the warm water spraying the excited researchers as they approached a soft shore littered with only fragments of drift wood and the rays of the afternoon sun. Eighteen in all, less the captain who remained on board as well as the mechanic who was fiddling about with some minor adjust to the engines, the researchers where here on their own device quite literally now as they embarked on their first landing on soil since driving the boat down nearly at full tilt almost two weeks ago from Key West. It was there that they had loaded up on nearly every imaginable supply, scientific or eatable, know to modern man.

Customs had been curtsied well in advance through undiplomatic channels at corporate headquarters to help ensure a quiet entry. Their presence was by no means illegal, indeed all of the necessary paperwork was dully on file, save perhaps for the real reason the crew had landed and of course the full extent of their work. Gleefully almost, the crew trappiezed their way around a dashing of volcanic boulders strewn close to the shoreline and gently eased on to the tan shore.

Tumbling waves crescendoed. The ocean could keep them at bay no longer. Even the mighty sea seemed to acquiesce. As their vessel screeched softly against the stand the waves lapped half-heartily against the shore. The water that bore them here retreated under their giddy feet, and a sea green enveloped them now. The wild was upon them as the full canopy glistened expectantly watching their landing. A thousand curious eyes in the jungle watched their landing. Scarlet macaws grouped in pairs darted from a nearby palm high into the sky, circled, then landed further up in the jungle. All around them the presence of the jungle captured their minds, but sadly their hearts seems destined for other, more sinister things.

♠ ♥ ♣ ♦

LAUREN QUICK-TIED A beach towel between the foliage in a makeshift changing screen. Her last dry item of clothing, a light gray t-shirt, landed on top of her khaki shorts. Rummaging through her dry-bag, Lauren found her swimsuit. She pulled up her polka-dotted bikini over her pale bottom and popped on the black top over her tan breasts. Only seconds after she whipped off her shorts and top, slow, slow seconds to Declan, the bikini was zipped over by a neoprene diving suit termed a "shorty" because it only covered up to her forearms and calves. Lauren emerged from the foliage and wound down to the sandy knoll. She grabbed her gear and motioned over to Declan.

Still groggy after his run-in, or perhaps better put run-out with the bull sharks, he clamored over to Lauren's canoe. He had numerous bouts of shooting pain running into his thighs, his chest, and apparently even his internal organs were not cooperating with him much either. He tumbled into her kayak.

Lauren helped ease his bulk inside the plastic shell. She had stripped the kayak of every comfort and stacked the remnants along with all her gear on the beach. From there she hog tied everything into the highest high-water tree along the banks. Lauren didn't know what would be left when, or if they returned, but she didn't really care at this point. Declan had survived the first 48 hours, it was now or never, to attempt a transport.

Lauren reminded herself to have a better back-up plan in place next time, the very fact that she routinely disappeared for weeks at a time hadn't occurred to her that this could have been her. But then again it wasn't her, she smiled, she was too wily to get in a jam like this. Thinking about it again she realized, actually she was in a jam now too. Lauren helped load Declan onboard, then she pushed off.

Her goal was simple, reach the Sirena ranger station and have them bring in help or transport him out. Either way, that was the best chance she had of moving him out. His blood loss had only stopped the day before and she had had just enough liquids to keep him hydrated. Declan was fully medicated now with enough pain relievers to stop a troupe of howler monkeys, but he showed no effects. At least it helped his complaining, that seemed to have slowed.

They were well into the second hour of the row when he began to vomit dark red blood that instantly aerated once it hit the water. He was chumming their trail and about the time she decided to row him in a scattering of fins appeared in their wake. This was going to be tricky because she couldn't out-paddle them and she couldn't stay bobbing in the ocean here either. She looked down at Declan. Apparently he wasn't well enough to travel. But what was she going to do? She still had another four hours paddle, at least, and he wouldn't have been able to help himself for another day.

"We have to pull in," she motioned to him using her thumb, "you're keeping them on us with that chum line of yours."

Declan leaned forward, looked at her, and vomited again. "I don't think this is going to turn out well."

They felt the first nudge on the boat, which almost capsized them.

"Those are some big boys. Probably the same ones in the cavern that got to me." Declan wiped his mouth with his forearm.

"Keep paddling," Declan moaned. He scanned the bottom of the kayak for the other paddle. She had hooked it under the plastic molding. Declan grunted in half, pulling his body up. He reached around his backside and unsheathed the dive knife.

"Declan, what are you doing? Help me paddle!" Lauren shouted.

She was making a great dash for shore, but the surf was tough and the breakers even tougher.

"Slap. Slap. Slap." She dug the oar into the sea and pushed forward. For a time she had the advantage over them. The bulls hated the surge. They swam under it. Lauren pushed ahead and tumbled over the crests. The breakers eased and she found herself in the shallow, eighty feet from shore in crystal clear water. Then they hit again.

The bulls, there were two big dorsal fins now, rushed the plastic kayak and flipped it. Lauren swung under the kayak and locked her hands around the undercarriage to keep afloat. She saw them quickly circle. And as they commenced the bite and drag sequence, the kayak jerked backward with a splashing white rush. Declan hit the water with the other oar outfitted like a harpoon, his knife hilt jacked into the oar's tube. He didn't even bother shaking and trying to fend off both monsters, rather he attacked the bull shark closest to the canoe.

It was over in a flash. Declan launched his entire body weight into the push and drove the blade in four feet behind the shark's left eye, into the gill complex. The gills shredded and bits of flesh filled the sea. The other bull whipped around and bit directly at the blood burst, missing Declan's abdomen by inches. The shark Declan hit was dead, but flinched in short spastic convulsions toward its wound in a defensive posture ultimately locking its jaws in a death grip on its rival. Jaw to jaw, they spiraled out to sea.

Declan grabbed the inverted plastic kayak and flipped it over. He wedged his arm into the lasso in front and kicked forward toward Lauren who was floating face down. He turned her sunny-side up and started rescue breathing. Kicking, kicking, kicking he made his way to standing ground and let the boat float away. He tilted Lauren forward and drained her. He kept at it until a violent cough triggered the gag reflex and Lauren bent to her side and vomited.

"Nice...that's both of us." Declan put his head back, exhausted.

"Can I convince you to walk it in from here?" Declan looked into her eyes, grabbed her head, and kissed Lauren on her forehead. She was taking deep, painful breaths that subsided into short gasps. She sat up and looked out on the water.

"You got both of them?" Her eyes followed the contours of the water and fell on the murky spot deep in the lagoon's shelter that was crimson.

"Just need to get one, figured his buddy would finish him off. No loyalty with sharks." Declan talked while looking up through the palm's shade loaded with coconuts.

"You thirsty?" He looked down towards Lauren. She had stood and was walking to the shoreline to get a bag that washed ashore.

"What's that?" If Declan remembered correctly, it was the waterproof food bag. Oh he was hungry.

"Allow me to buy you lunch." Lauren unhitched the waterproof canary yellow scuba bag and pulled out four browned bananas and a Zip-Lock bag full of chocolate chips cookies.

"You got to be kidding me...chocolate chip cookies?" Declan propped himself up against the coconut tree.

"Oh yes, I was going to use these to bribe you to get off the boat at Sirena...but I think we're due for a little treat now."

"Mmmm...I'd say." Declan leaned back against the tree and closed his eyes. The afternoon sun felt so, so good on his body. Black and blue, his abdomen continued to swell. His legs weren't looking that good either, yet he slept. Lauren unzipped the wetsuit shorty and put her bikini back on in front of Declan.

She kissed Declan on his forehead. "Oh my little jungle diver," she thought.

Lauren unzipped the wetsuit shortly and wrapped the wetsuit around her waist, then the coconut tree. She preceded a-la-telephone man up the tree. By the time dusk came, she had built a camp complete with fire and some forty coconuts. Declan came and went into consciousness, but on the setting of the sun he popped back into the world.

"Looks good...what's for dinner? Banana-cookie casserole?" Declan looked around. "Hey Lauren," he motioned her over. "Can you feel what this is?"

Declan pulled his bandage, a torn and tied t-shirt, up and moved Lauren's hand along his stomach. It bumped against a swollen protrusion. The soft mass was burning hot. Upon closer inspection it smelled awful. Declan judged by her reaction that this wasn't good. Hell, he knew that this wasn't good. "Lauren, what do you know about medicine?"

She looked up at him with tears in her eyes and looked away. "Declan, it's your intestine all swollen up."

Declan looked at her and smiled. "Well hold the bananas in my casserole then!" She didn't laugh. "Lauren, get some of the salt water and clean the wound again please. Do we have enough coconut milk to drink?"

Lauren brought her head up again to look at him. "Yeah Declan we have enough to drink. And I can dress your bandage again. But that's not going to help, is it?"

He looked at her and paused. "No, probably not for too long, but long enough I think for you to get over to Sirena."

"Declan even if I get to Sirena and we all come back for you, you still will have to go to San Jose. We're still two days away from real help."

Declan looked away from her toward the horizon. He grinned and shook his head. "It's beautiful here, isn't it?" He smiled at Lauren.

"Damn it, Declan we need help now!" She found herself screaming at him. A sharp snap sounded in the distance. Then another. Then another. In the matter of moments four large men looking like they just came out of a hunting catalog stumbled upon them.

"Who needs help?" The leader of the group asked, fully out-of-breath in perfect English. He leaned forward.

Declan read the nametag embroidered on his vest "Dr. Stan Vlacik, Lead Scientist, *Modern Explorer*."

♠ ♥ ♣ ♦

A HANDFUL OF blue-green marbles fell on the walnut desk, snapped up sharply, then began to roll each in their own direction. Travis Smiley anchored his broad back into the upholstered leather chair. His eyes followed the marbles along the grains of the walnut watching intently as they made their way down the long planks with some falling off the edge, while others persisted in their journey.

He was alone in the boardroom, fifteen minutes early for the weekly meeting with his directors. They were a motley crew of select businessmen and woman that were supposed to be representing the interests of the company's shareholders. Their sole purpose was to act on the behalf of shareholders, to diligently look at the executive management of the company, with if not a magnifying glass surely not a telescope either. This proved to be difficult for the board of IPEEC given that they were all appointed by the executive committee.

Twelve directors filled the IPEEC boardroom at two o'clock, greeting each other informally with warm, caring handshakes tanned with the sun of a golf course and softened by the yachtsman's sea. Smiley sat at the head of the twelve, with the highest backed chair facing the board and beyond them he could pier out the glass and steel architecture into the wild world outside. The boardroom was tastefully decorated with several Warhols, a double-back of library books, and a meticulously groomed Japanese garden in each of the four corners.

Travis thumbed his marbles retrieved from the seats and beige carpeted flooring. He held them in his hands and rolled the glass spheres in circles around each other.

"Fellow directors we are at a decision point. Do we begin drilling operations or not? Our scientific survey team has affirmed the previous field data. El Tigre is a viable project, one that requires our decisive input." Smiley stared down the long polished table and let his comments seep into the very groves of the wood.

"Mr. Smiley," a thin blonde woman with an exceptionally well-cut St. John's suit addressed the board through him, "does the team know yet that we'll have to float a rig off the coast?"

"No, no they don't. But given the brainpower we sent down to the site it won't be long before they realize a land-based operation is next to impossible. At that point we most likely will alienate several of the team due to their conservative environmental beliefs. It doesn't matter though, because we'll have them pulled out long before we send in the extraction team to establish the beachhead and initial light terminal construction."

Smiley looked at and through the board while he spoke. He knew that after the advance team learned of the full implications of the survey results he would have a revolt on his hands. Smiley frowned and rolled the marbles in his hand nervously one over another.

♠ ♥ ♣ ♦

CLEAR, TEMPERATE WATER began to cloud. It reflected the sky above. The soft lapping waves grew to tumblers, and most notable of all, the jungle became quiet. The wind picked up over the next couple hours. Already the birds had left their perches and sought higher ground. The small mammals, rodents and the like, gave away their lairs and also sought safety higher in the hills. And the apex predators stopped their hunts, which they never did, and sought shelter. A tempest ultimately started as the collection of breezes joined together.

The beach became deafening and the sky alive. Alive with the heart-stopping crackle of thunder ignited by lightening tearing through the sky like a jagged knife. Cutting, and turning, and tearing the sky into fragments of air. It exploded, then reloaded.

"Kaboom!" Again the sky flashed.

"Smash!"

St. Elmo's fire lined the eves of the horizon and a smell of anarchy scented the air. Coconuts took flight like launched cannon balls. Snapping trees couldn't be heard because of the crashing surf. It churned the sea floor over and upon itself. The soft talc beach sandblasted the rocky shore.

Salvador Maria Antonio stood up to his waist in the river against the ocean's edge, with his palms pressing down against the surging water. He reached into the soul of the water. He stood as if he was a product of nature, a piece of the whole born in the surf, raised in the jungle and not of humanity, but rather a spirit of Corcovado taken the shape of man.

The rain pelted his exposed chest. He let it run down his face, over his shoulders, and down his arms. Salvador Maria Antonio was at one with the world. The crew of *Modern Explorer* looked on in disbelief.

This was the man summoned to help escort Pickle's patch-job back to the world. A patch-job requiring no less than two hundred stitches and three transfusions of the artificial blood they kept stocked. He would be well kept to keep off his feet for the foreseeable future. A diagnosis Pickle had no doubt Declan would ignore. This cat was on his fourth life, and Pickle suspected he'd burn through all nine in due course. Pickle looked over and saw Lauren still hovering above Declan. She moved to the bow and waved ashore. And this is who came. Lauren greeted Salvador Maria Antonio heartily, knowing full well what was at stake.

Salvador Maria Antonio weathered the storm with the crew of *Modern Explorer*, and in the morning looked in on Declan in his sleeping chamber. Mooring in the sheltered cove probably saved the vessel that night. The breakers couldn't consummate the full sea, only the wind's rush made it past.

Pickle and his crew had done a remarkable job cleaning Declan up. Salvador Maria Antonio sat shoeless on a tee-pee stool and rubbed his forehead in contemplative admiration. He wasn't wearing any shoes because he had checked his rubber boots upon entry onto the vessel. Like everything else on this vessel he soon discovered had a purpose, function, and specific place. Declan was comfortably propped up. His organs were repacked, stitched, and bandaged. Salvador Maria Antonio's eyes wandered around the little stateroom. The room was pleasant enough, rich with a small library and the floor was carpeted with a thick beige rug. Above Declan's bunk he could see out the portholes at the day.

"Salvador Maria Antonio?" Lauren had come into the room.

"Shhh…," he motioned as he stood up and walked with Lauren topside. "Declan has a pretty nice recovery room."

"He sure does." Lauren looked across the catamaran and let her gaze stop on the shore. "Looks to me like the crew is out and about exploring for something even more precious. Am I right?"

"You are." Salvador Maria Antonio followed her gaze. "I think their expedition hit a roadblock though. Only a week into it all and they're starting to realize what the company that sent them down here really wants to accomplish."

"Sure is one thing to plan a rig on paper, quite another to put one in once you've experienced Corcovado, isn't it?" Lauren let her eyes fall on Salvador Maria Antonio.

"It is." Salvador Maria Antonio's voice was a whisper.

Declan was immobilized for the better part of a week. It made no sense at this point to move him, the clinic on board *Modern Explorer* rivaled his care in San Jose. He spent the end of the week topside playing cards with the crew as each member rotated in and out of the jungle.

The teams came back exhausted, raw, and starving. Salvador Maria Antonio had dedicated himself to an unusual task, he voluntarily took them into the furthest reaches of the park and along with several of his guides gave the tour of their lives. He made it quite apparent what was at stake and also the lengths to which he would risk everything he had to protect this preserve. Degreed intellectuals, rough practitioners, and eventually the champion of both, Pickle, came singularly to the same conclusion. They could not let this plan pass, in any form.

What had started out as an expedition to confirm the petroleum reserves now became an operation to seize *Modern Explorer* for their own use in preventing the establishment from gaining access to this paradise. Rarely in the annuals of environmental action has such a decidedly single-purpose goal changed so dramatically. *Modern Explorer* became their floating base of operations. It was mutually agreed by the crew, Salvador Maria Antonio, and his re-found explorer Declan that they would work in unison to prevent any encroachment. Salvador Maria Antonio used his influence at the Tico Times. Lauren gathered support through her academic channels. Declan decided to take care of some unfinished business in San Jose.

Salvador Maria Antonio knew better than any of them, and as conversations ran into the night, and Corcovado shook every man to his soul with yet another evening storm, Salvador Maria Antonio swayed the team first from shock, to realization, and finally to agreeable action. So they planned and plotted. This would be a fight unlike any of the team ever fought before.

♠ ♥ ♣ ♦

He palmed the bar of gold loosely. It felt cool in his hands. Months of dredging, surviving two near-death treks back through the jungle, and countless stitches yielded a rectangular bar of gold compact as a pack of cigarettes, but weighing a kilogram. All his prospecting and mining work collecting the fluvial gold smelted down to a single bar. Declan admired his handy-work.

Noticeable impurities remained, but for a home-processing job the bar came out well. Indeed, it was worth a quarter million dollars. His workbench was cluttered with the smelting equipment and a host of older texts, some in English and some in Spanish. They were yellowed, perhaps gilded, with exposure to the sun and spotted from drops of sweat in the furnace room. He knew what had to be done; the sports betting operation had been dismantled, employees paid, and the shop closed. Declan was able to sell the telephone number, 1-800-BET-ONIT, for a cool $10,000. He had amassed over half a million dollars in his business banking account.

All of Declan's business funds were funneled to Salvador Maria Antonio and the rangers. They would be waging a literal guerilla war against the inbound oil company. Apparently a team of mercenaries had been hired to help "clean out" any initial resistance by IPEEC. This wasn't necessarily a surprise. What was, however, was that the original advance team from the oil company had sided with the rangers. Call it what you will, but the proverbial tipping point in every man's soul had been reached. Their information and knowledge of the park's natural resources would prove to be extremely valuable in defending Corcovado. But the wheels of war were in motion and what hung in the balance was pristine nature, irreplaceable and priceless. Their success hinged seemingly more on luck than anything else. Against overwhelming odds, they were willing to try and catch a falling leaf.

Declan loaded the full extent of his gear in the chartered plane to Drake Bay. It bulged at the riveted seams. He had enough gear to stay in-country for six months. With the rangers' assistance Declan unloaded and ported the gear across the bay and toward Corcovado, stopping only along the way to greet Salvador Maria Antonio at Sirena and meet up with Lauren. They left the majority of the gear at Sirena, repacked the remaining equipment with them, and took off into the heart of the jungle.

Lauren and Declan established camp with a full complement of supplies along the shores of Corcovado's highest peak, El Tigre. Even Tucker in Colorado Springs decided to throw his full complement of technology behind them. He would provide the overhead support, from communications to logistics.

Declan held Lauren's hand loosely as he walked across the sand. This would be their base of operations. Their team was assembled here; already the mutinous crew of the *Modern Explorer* had gone inland to establish a beachhead. Here in the heart of Corcovado, where the fresh jungle river kissed the sea, where the wealth of nations silently flowed below them, Declan let the gold bar slip back into her leafy, wise hands.